He'd been a heartbeat away from kissing her.

Another second and he would have. She'd seen it in his eyes. For a moment, at least, he hadn't been seeing her brother's little sister or the child she'd been. He'd seen her as a woman.

And he'd wanted her. Colleen could feel the imprint of Gun's hand on her skin, as if branded there.

She looked at him from under her lashes. He was so close. She had only to stretch out her hand to be able to bury her fingers in the thick gold of his hair.

The hard set of his jaw kept her from giving in to that temptation. Gun might have wanted her, but he didn't like it.

She'd better give him some time to get used to the idea.

Dear Reader,

Welcome to another month of fine reading from Silhouette Intimate Moments. And what better way to start off the month than with an American Hero title from Marilyn Pappano, a book that's also the beginning of a new miniseries, Southern Knights. Hero Michael Bennett and his friends Remy and Smith are all dedicated to upholding the law—and to loving the right lady. And in *Michael's Gift*, she turns out to be the one woman he wishes she wasn't. To know more, you'll just have to read this terrific story.

The month continues with *Snow Bride*, the newest from bestselling writer Dallas Schulze. Then it's on to *Wild Horses, Wild Men*, from Ann Williams; *Waking Nightmare*, from highly regarded newcomer Alicia Scott; *Breaking the Rules*, Ruth Wind's Intimate Moments debut; and *Hear No Evil*, a suspenseful novel from brand-new author Susan Drake. I think you'll enjoy each and every one of these books—and that you'll be looking for more equally exciting reading next month and in the months to come. So look no further than Silhouette Intimate Moments, where, each and every month, we're proud to bring you writers we consider among the finest in the genre today.

Enjoy!

Leslie J. Wainger
Senior Editor and Editorial Coordinator

Please address questions and book requests to:
Silhouette Reader Service
U.S.: 3010 Walden Ave., P.O. Box 1325, Buffalo, NY 14269
Canadian: P.O. Box 609, Fort Erie, Ont. L2A 5X3

SNOW

BRIDE

Dallas Schulze

Silhouette®
INTIMATE™ MOMENTS®

Published by Silhouette Books

America's Publisher of Contemporary Romance

SILHOUETTE BOOKS

ISBN 0-373-07584-7

SNOW BRIDE

Copyright © 1994 by Dallas Schulze

This edition published by arrangement with Harlequin Enterprises B. V.

® and TM are trademarks of Harlequin Enterprises B. V., used under
license. Trademarks indicated with ® are registered in the United States
Patent and Trademark Office, the Canadian Trade Marks Office and in
other countries.

Printed in U.S.A.

Books by Dallas Schulze

Silhouette Intimate Moments

Moment to Moment #170
Donovan's Promise #247
The Vow #318
The Baby Bargain #377
Everything but Marriage #414
The Hell-Raiser #462
Secondhand Husband #500
Michael's Father #565
Snow Bride #584

Silhouette Books

Birds, Bees and Babies 1994
"Cullen's Child"

DALLAS SCHULZE

loves books, old movies, her husband and her cat, not necessarily in that order. A sucker for a happy ending, her writing has given her an outlet for her imagination. Dallas hopes that readers have half as much fun with her books as she does! She has more hobbies than there is space to list them, but is currently working on a doll collection. Dallas loves to hear from her readers, and you can write to her at P.O. Box 241, Verdugo City, CA 91046.

Chapter 1

She was going to die.

Colleen Bryan braced one hand against the trunk of a sturdy pine tree and stared at the swirling whiteness that surrounded her, cutting her field of vision to almost nothing. She shivered under the bite of the wind that sliced through the fabric of her coat. She wasn't dressed for a blizzard. But then she hadn't expected to encounter one this late in the year.

When it comes to Wyoming weather, it's best not to have expectations.

Her father's voice was so clear in her mind that Colleen peered through the falling snow, half expecting to see his tall figure standing nearby. But Patrick Bryan had been dead for eight years. She blinked snow-crusted lashes and forced her sluggish thoughts to clarity.

She was going to die. The thought drifted through her mind again, accompanied, not by fear, but by a vague indifference, as if it had no real meaning. She was so tired. It seemed as if she'd been struggling for days, though it couldn't have been more than a few hours at most.

She'd awakened to the snow, to a layer of white drifted over her sleeping bag, as soft as goose down but not nearly as warm. She might not have been prepared for a blizzard, but she'd spent all her life in Wyoming, and she recognized the danger in that deceptively gentle snowfall, in the heavy cloud cover overhead. She'd known she couldn't reach her car and that there was a cabin nearby. If she could reach that...

But it was starting to get difficult to remember *why* she was fighting so hard. It would be so much easier to lie down in the nice, soft snow and just go to sleep. It looked warm, like a fluffy, white blanket, and she was cold, so very cold.

Mesmerized by the layer of white at her feet, Colleen took a half step forward, thinking to lie down in the hollow she could see just ahead. The snow would be thicker and softer there, like sinking into a feather mattress. She took another step and her foot nearly slid out from under her. The sudden jolt as she caught herself sent a sharp pain stabbing through her left leg. She grabbed a thick pine bough to keep herself from falling.

Colleen stood still for a moment, her breath coming in quick gasps as she waited for the ache to subside. The pain had cut through the fuzziness in her head like a warm knife going through butter. The snow no longer looked warm and inviting. It looked cold and deadly. She knew if she lay down, if she fell, she wouldn't get up. She would die here on this mountain. And she didn't want to die.

Of course, she might not have a choice, she thought with a sudden flash of black humor. But she was damned if she was going to lie down and let her life seep away. If the storm wanted her, it was going to have to fight for her.

Colleen forced herself away from the tree and stumbled forward. She deliberately put more weight on her left leg, welcoming the resulting pain as a reminder that she was alive, using it as a prod to keep struggling. It was the first time in the five years since the accident that she'd had reason to be grateful for the injury and the weakness it had left behind.

The cabin couldn't be far, she told herself. Once she reached it, she'd be all right. There was a little potbellied stove inside and there was always wood left on the porch. She could get warm again, wait out the storm. Peering through the falling snow, Colleen tried to push aside the knowledge that, in this kind of weather, she could pass within a few yards of the little building and not see it.

She tripped on a rock hidden under the snow and went to her knees. Pain lanced up her leg, sharp enough to make her cry out, the sound startling in the pale silence around her. She stayed where she was for a moment, on her hands and knees in the snow, forcing the pain down, refusing to consider the possibility that her leg might not support her.

If she couldn't get up, she'd die. It was that simple. And since she'd already decided she didn't want to die, she'd just have to get up. Pure willpower got her to her feet. Stubbornness, her brother, Kel, would have said.

Kel. Longing for his strong presence almost brought Colleen to her knees again. Why hadn't she told him she was going to spend some time camping in the mountains that formed the northern boundaries of the ranch? If he knew she was out here, he would already have people out looking for her. But he didn't know. No one knew. She'd very carefully arranged it so that no one would miss her for at least a month. She'd wanted time to herself, time to think about her future.

Well, that shouldn't take long, she thought as she stumbled again and grabbed for a tree trunk to keep from falling. It looked as if her future might be considerably shorter than she'd expected. Her face was too cold to smile at the bleak humor of that thought.

The ache in her leg was constant now, worse than it had been since she'd broken it five years ago. She shuffled forward a few feet. The line between past and present began to blur. Was she on the mountain, struggling through the snow, or was she lying at the bottom of a gully, her leg shattered, her horse dead and Gun leaning over her, his face white and set?

Gun. Was Gun with her? She turned her head, looking for his large figure. But there was nothing but snow and trees. Tears of disappointment stung Colleen's eyes. She wouldn't have to be afraid if Gun were with her. Hadn't he promised long ago that he'd never let anything happen to her?

She'd been eight years old when she'd climbed to the top of a windmill, only to discover that going up was a lot easier than contemplating getting back down. It had been Gun who'd climbed up to get her. At twenty-four, he'd been tall, blond and godlike. When she'd started to cry with fear, he'd held her against his chest and told her not to be scared because he'd never let anything happen to her.

She'd decided then that she was going to marry him when she grew up. And she'd seen no reason to change her mind in the intervening sixteen years, despite the fact that he still seemed to see her as that eight-year-old child.

Colleen leaned against a tree, fighting the urge to cry as every breath of icy air seemed to cut into her aching lungs. At the moment, Gun would be welcome to treat her like a child. He could even scold her for her stupidity if only he were here. It wasn't that she couldn't take care of herself, she thought. It was just that there were moments when a little help would be appreciated.

Staying too long in one place could be fatal, she reminded herself. She pushed away from the tree. Her feet were so cold she couldn't feel them anymore. Had she taken a step or was she standing still? She forced her leg forward. Didn't she? Yes, that was right, she was walking, walking. But if she was walking, why could she feel the snow crunching beneath the fabric of her gloves?

She stared stupidly at the ground beneath her, slowly realizing that she'd once again fallen to her hands and knees. She shouldn't be on her hands and knees, she thought crossly. She wouldn't be able to travel very far that way. She had to get up again.

Sheer determination got her upright and carried her another half dozen steps. She'd lost her sense of direction. The cabin could have been directly in front of her or she could have already passed it. She no longer thought about it. She just had to keep moving. If she kept moving, she'd... She couldn't quite remember just what would happen. But she knew she had to keep moving.

Her left knee buckled and Colleen felt herself start to fall. It seemed to happen almost in slow motion, giving her plenty of time to realize that she'd never make it back onto her feet again. She was too cold, too bone-deep weary. When she hit the ground this time, that's where she'd stay.

She stared at the snow, watching it come up to meet her, and then an iron bar seemed to catch her across the stomach, halting her fall, driving the air from her. In the next heartbeat, the world was spinning around her as her feet were swept out from under her and she felt herself brought against the hard strength of a man's chest.

Though her eyelids felt too heavy to lift, she forced them upward and stared into her rescuer's face. A black ski mask covered his features, leaving only his eyes exposed. Blue eyes, the color of a summer sky. She hadn't seen those eyes in nearly three years, but she knew them as well as her own.

"Gun." Colleen thought she said his name out loud, but she wasn't sure. She couldn't hear the sound of her voice over the sudden sound of the wind. Or was that rushing noise only in her head? She turned her face into the fabric of his coat, letting herself go lax with a prayer that he wasn't a figment of her imagination.

Gunnar Larsen felt Colleen go slack in his arms and fear stopped his heart. But the steady rise and fall of her chest reassured him. She'd just passed out. And no wonder, he thought. God alone knew how long she'd been out in the middle of the blizzard. And not exactly dressed for it, either, he thought, his eyes skimming over the jeans and hiking boots and heavy jacket that she wore. It'd be a miracle if she didn't end up with frostbite.

Holding her close against his chest, he turned toward the cabin. Its sturdy outlines were barely visible through the falling snow. Soft white flakes were already filling in the wavering trail of footprints she'd left in the snow, but a quick glance told him that she'd been headed away from the cabin. If he hadn't been feeling restless and decided to check on his horse... Gun's arms tightened protectively around the woman he held.

Colleen stirred as she heard the sound of boot heels thudding against worn wooden planks. She hadn't blacked out completely, only let herself drift off, relieved that she didn't have to struggle anymore. Gun had her safe and sound and she didn't really care whether he was real or not.

But the blast of heat that struck her chilled skin was definitely real, painfully so. She caught her breath, her eyes flying open as Gun carried her into the cabin she'd been struggling to reach. He caught the door with the toe of his boot and swung it shut behind them, closing out the storm.

Gun didn't slow his stride as he carried her across the cabin's single room. Colleen had a quick impression of log walls decorated with woven blankets, and the smell of coffee. She gasped as Gun opened his arms and dumped her unceremoniously onto the narrow bed that sat in one corner of the room.

"Just what the hell were you doing out there?" he demanded angrily.

Colleen blinked up at him and decided that if he were a figment of her imagination he wouldn't be shouting at her. He yanked off the ski mask, the better to glare at her. Though she'd known him all her life, she was struck again by the sheer masculine beauty of him. From the tousled thickness of his pale blond hair to the chiseled strength of his chin, she'd never in her life seen a man more calculated to send a woman's blood pressure soaring.

"Were you trying to kill yourself?" he demanded when she didn't say anything.

Neither the fact that he was gorgeous nor the fact that she'd intended to marry him since she was eight years old gave him a right to raise his voice to her.

"Don't shout at me," she said firmly. Or it would have been firm if her teeth hadn't begun to chatter like castanets.

Hearing the cranky command, Gun felt some of the tension ease out of him. When she'd just sat there staring at him with that dazed look in her big green eyes, he'd started to worry. But the temper in her voice reassured him. Even when she was a little girl, she'd had a temper to match the red in her hair. If she was snapping at him, she was going to be all right.

"Get out of those clothes," he told her as he turned away. Shrugging out of his coat, he tossed it in the general direction of the door where pegs had been driven into a log to provide coat hangers. He'd hang it up later. What mattered now was getting Colleen warm.

Grabbing a rag to protect his hand, he pulled open the door on the little cast-iron stove and tossed a few more chunks of wood on the bed of coals in its belly. He'd made coffee earlier, leaving the battered aluminum pot on the back of the stove to keep warm. By now the brew inside was probably strong enough to strip paint, but it was hot and that was all that mattered.

"Get some of this inside you," he said, turning back to Colleen. She was sitting on the edge of the bed, just where he'd left her. "I told you to get out of those clothes," he snapped. She'd pulled off the lime green knit cap that had covered her head and now she glared up at him from beneath a tangle of bright auburn hair.

"Don't shout at me." Her chattering teeth gave the words a staccato rhythm.

"I'm not shouting."

"Yes, you are." Her eyes were bright green against her pale skin. "I'm cold, not deaf," she added peevishly.

"I wasn't shouting." Gun stopped and drew a deep breath, aware that, while he might not have been shouting, he'd definitely raised his voice. He'd never known anyone who could rile his temper faster than Colleen Bryan. His fingers tightened over the thick ceramic mug. "I'm not shouting," he said again in a carefully controlled voice.

"You were."

If that wasn't just like her—never back down, never give up an argument. She had a stubborn streak a mile wide and it had been there ever since she was a baby.

"Well, I'm not shouting now. I'm asking you very politely to get out of those damp clothes before you end up with pneumonia. *If* you wouldn't mind too terribly much," he added in a tone so far from a shout that it was an insult.

She glared at him a moment longer and then lowered her eyes, but not before he'd caught the shimmer of tears in them.

"I can't work the zipper," she admitted.

Of course she couldn't. She wouldn't be able to grip anything as small as a zipper tab with her chilled fingers. She must have used her teeth to pull her gloves off. Cursing his own stupidity for not having realized she'd need help, Gun crouched down in front of her and reached for the recalcitrant zipper.

Colleen clenched her jaw to try to control the chattering of her teeth and stared at the thick lock of pale gold hair that fell onto Gun's forehead. If she'd been able to feel her fingers, she would have been tempted to lift them and brush his hair back from his face. And probably get her hand smacked for her trouble, she thought as Gun tugged the coat off her shoulders. She wasn't sure he'd even noticed that she wasn't the pigtailed little girl who'd tagged so annoyingly after him and Kel. He tossed her coat across the foot of the bed.

"What are you doing?" She batted at his hands as he reached for the hem of the heather gray crew-neck sweater she'd worn under her coat.

"I'm getting you out of these wet clothes," he said, his brows lifting in surprise.

"I can handle it from here." The words would have sounded more definite if her teeth hadn't started chattering again right in the midst of them.

"Sure you can." He reached for the sweater and she smacked his hand again.

"You're not undressing me, Gun Larsen!"

"For crying out loud, it's not like I haven't seen you without clothes before," he snapped, exasperated.

"Not since I was five years old." She glared at him until he threw his hands up in exasperation.

"Fine. Do it yourself." He stood and put his hands on his hips, waiting.

"Turn your back!" The chattering of her teeth was threatening to expand into body-racking shivers, but she refused to give an inch.

"It's turned."

He faced away from her, muttering under his breath about stubborn females with the temperaments of wolverines. He stared at the opposite wall and listened to the rustling sounds behind him. She was behaving like an idiot, of course. Like he'd said, he'd seen her naked before. Okay, so she wasn't five anymore, but she was still Kel's baby sister. Which put her just about as far off-limits as a nun. He just wanted to get her out of her wet clothes and under the covers. It wasn't as if he had plans to seduce her, for goodness' sake. Hell, she might not be five, but she was still just a kid.

A frustrated sob brought him around to face her again. The gray sweater lay in a damp heap on the floor, but the button at the top of her jeans had defeated her. And even if she could have gotten the jeans undone, he didn't know how she'd planned on unlacing her boots.

Without giving Colleen a chance to argue, Gun sank back down in front of her and unlaced her boots with quick efficient jerks. He tugged them off and then peeled off the wet woolen socks. Her feet were icy, but there was no sign of frostbite, he noted with relief. Ignoring her angry look, he stood, pulling her up with him before unfastening her jeans.

It wasn't until he began stripping the damp denim down her legs that it occurred to him that Colleen might be his best friend's baby sister, but she was definitely *not* a child anymore. He eased the stiff fabric over her hips and swallowed hard. She was, most emphatically, a woman. And this was a hell of a time to notice that fact!

Colleen stared down at Gun's head as he knelt at her feet. Her fantasies had put him there many times, but this wasn't exactly the way she'd envisioned it. White cotton panties and a matching cotton chemise were a far cry from black silk and lace. And there should have been candlelight and maybe satin sheets, not gray daylight and log walls.

"Sit down so I can pull these off." His voice sounded a little more gruff than usual. He brought his hands up, clasping her hips to ease her back down onto the bed, and Colleen sucked in a sharp breath. It must be the fact that her skin was so cold that made his hands feel so hot against her skin.

The minute she was sitting down, Gun pulled his hands away, feeling as if he'd just taken hold of a hot coal. He didn't look at her as he pulled her jeans down over her slender legs. He must have been alone too long. That was the only possible explanation for this sudden awareness of little Colleen Bryan as a woman. *Not so little,* he amended, his fingers lingering on one shapely calf. He couldn't remember the last time he'd seen a nicer pair of legs. Legs like that made a man think of things like how narrow that bed was and what a tight fit it would be for two people.

Tight fit. The two words conjured up other images and Gun jerked his fingers away from Colleen's leg as if it had suddenly caught fire.

"Get under the covers," he said gruffly. Standing, he made a point of draping her jeans over the back of a chair. When he turned around, he was grateful to see that she was modestly covered from toes to chin. Big green eyes watched him from over the edge of the faded gray blanket. Despite her best efforts at control, he could see the shivers that raced through her.

"The best thing for you would be a warm bath, but I'm afraid the local facilities don't run to that."

"I'll have to complain to the concierge," she said through chattering teeth.

Gun grinned. "You do that. But while he's looking into the problem, why don't you see if you can get some of this coffee down you. It's strong enough to float a horseshoe."

"Complete with horse?" she asked, echoing her sister-in-law's complaints about ranch coffee.

"Complete with horse," Gun promised, smiling at the reminder of Megan's description of the brew.

In the end, Colleen was shivering too much to control the cup on her own. Gun perched on the side of the bed, supporting her with one arm behind her back while he fed her careful sips of hot coffee. The soft curves pressed against his side chased away the last, lingering images of the pigtailed little girl who'd tagged along behind him and Kel.

Damn, when had she grown up? Gun steadied the mug as she took another drink and tried not to notice how silky soft her fiery hair felt where it brushed his cheek. She must be what? Nineteen? Twenty? He frowned and tried to keep his eyes from dropping to where the thin cotton of her chemise clung to the high curves of her breasts. She had to be more than twenty. He was forty. That meant she must be at least twenty-three, maybe twenty-four. Not exactly jailbait, but still too young for a man his age. Not that that was relevant, he reminded himself hastily. Even if she were older, she was still Kel's little sister. And still strictly off-limits.

By the time the coffee was gone, Colleen had nearly stopped shivering. She swallowed a sigh of regret as Gun withdrew the support of his arm and stood. It had almost been worth nearly freezing to death to have him hold her. And being snuggled against his big body had done at least as much to warm her up as the coffee.

She watched through sleepy eyes as he went to the window and twitched aside the curtain to look outside.

"Is it still snowing?"

"Like it plans on doing it for quite a while," he said. The idea didn't seem to please him.

Colleen yawned. Now that she was safely out of it, the snow was welcome to do as it pleased. She was dry and almost warm and with Gun. As far as she was concerned, that put her world in pretty decent shape. Gun turned to look at her just as she yawned again.

"You're not going to sleep," he ordered. His brows hooked together in a frown.

"I do not have hypothermia."

"Good. You're still not going to sleep. Not for a few hours at least."

"I'm fine." How could she have forgotten his annoying tendency to treat her as if she was still six years old?

"Then you won't mind staying awake," he noted.

Colleen barely resisted the urge to thrust her lower lip out in a pout. There were moments when she wondered if, instead of marrying Gun Larsen, she might not prefer to strangle him. But when she looked at him, she knew strangulation was not what she had in mind.

Wearing a pair of worn jeans and a blue buffalo check flannel shirt that echoed the color of his eyes, Gun was devastatingly attractive. At six foot four, he was as tall as her brother but more massively built. In her teens, she'd fancied that he looked like a Viking. It was easy to picture him standing at the helm of a dragon boat or wielding a heavy broadsword in battle. Or—her favorite image—carrying off maidens with auburn hair and green eyes.

"So you want to tell me what you were doing dressed for a day at the beach and wandering around in the middle of a blizzard," Gun asked.

"I was hardly dressed for the beach," she protested. "Unless it was in Greenland. And I wasn't expecting a blizzard this late in the year."

"This is Wyoming. You should—"

"I know. Expect the unexpected."

"I was going to say, be prepared. Like the Boy Scout motto."

"I wasn't a Boy Scout," she reminded him, watching as he opened a can of soup and dumped it into a battered aluminum pot.

"I can see that." Gun slanted her a quick, teasing look as he carried the pan over to the stove and set it on the single burner. "If they'd let girls as pretty as you in, *I* might have joined."

So he thought she was pretty. Colleen liked that. But she would have liked it more if the comment had been made in a less avuncular tone. *That* was the attitude she needed to get past if she was ever going to make Gun see her as something more than his best friend's little sister.

She yawned again, caught Gun's warning glance and resisted the urge to stick her tongue out at him—definitely not the way to show him she was all grown up. You'd think that after not seeing her for three years, he might have noticed that she was not a little girl anymore.

While the soup warmed, he went to the window again and frowned at the falling snow. Though he didn't say anything, Colleen knew he was thinking about the fact that they could find themselves snowed in. She blinked and sat up a little straighter, feeling her sleepiness fall from her.

Snowed in. With Gun. Just the two of them. For heaven knew how long.

Her mouth curved in a smile. If she couldn't make him notice her as a woman when they were snowed in together, then she didn't deserve to have him. Gun turned away from the window, his expression grim, and it was all Colleen could do to keep from laughing out loud.

Chapter 2

"You never did tell me what you were doing crawling around on the mountain," Gun said, returning to the stove to stir the soup.

"I wasn't crawling," Colleen said.

"No?" He glanced at her from under arched brows. "Looked a lot like crawling to me."

"Maybe I was examining the snowpack."

"Checking to see what the water supply might be like when it melts?"

"It's possible."

"Anything's possible," he agreed. "It's just that some things aren't very likely."

Colleen considered throwing a pillow at him, but she'd gotten them settled in just the right position behind her back. Besides which, the soup smelled good and it felt so nice to be in here with Gun rather than out in the cold that she couldn't find the energy to be annoyed by his teasing.

"Did anyone ever suggest that you're a nasty, cynical sort?" she asked, without real heat.

"It's been mentioned a time or two. Are you hungry?"

"Starved."

His mouth quirked at her fervent response. She sounded just like the Colleen he remembered, the one who would track him down when he was mending a fence and "share" his lunch with him. The memory of that freckle-faced twelve-year-old was reassuring until he turned and saw Colleen sitting on his bed, the gray blanket slipping provocatively down one creamy shoulder, her hair tumbling around a face that bore only a passing resemblance to the child he remembered.

He cleared his throat and resolutely looked away. "I'll get you something to put on."

The cabin didn't boast anything as elaborate as a closet, but years before someone had pounded a row of nails into one of the logs. Gun lifted a thick green plaid flannel shirt from a nail and brought it to Colleen.

"Thank you."

To his dismay, she let the blanket drop to her lap so that she could slip on the shirt. The rib-knit chemise she wore was certainly more modest than a lot of things he'd seen women wearing on the street, he reminded himself. But the reminder was not as effective as he would have liked. Particularly when it became obvious that her fingers were still too stiff to maneuver buttons through buttonholes.

"Let me do that." At her frustrated mutter, he crouched down beside the bed and pushed her hands aside. The sooner he had her safely buttoned into his shirt, the better for his peace of mind.

"I feel like a three-year-old," she said, frustrated.

Gun only wished that were true. But he could feel the soft curves of her breasts against the backs of his fingers, making him fumble as he tried to slip buttons through buttonholes that were suddenly impossibly small. *She's Kel's little sister,* he reminded himself. No matter that she didn't look like *anybody's* little sister, she was strictly off-limits. He rolled the shirt's sleeves up to free her hands and stood, moving away as quickly as he could without being obvious about it.

"I'll get you some soup and you can tell me what you're doing up here. Does Kel know you're here?" He swung back to look at her as the thought occurred to him. If Kel knew she was out in this storm, he'd be worried sick.

"No. Nobody does." Colleen's mouth twisted ruefully. "I wanted to be alone to think."

"You went camping without telling anyone where you'd be?" His brows, a darker shade than his hair, hooked together. "Do you know how stupid that was?"

"Yes."

The flat answer threw him off-balance. He'd already lined up several blistering comments, but he could hardly deliver them now. He settled for throwing her a stern look. "You could have died."

"I know. When I realized it was more than a flurry, I figured this cabin would be my best chance."

"You'd gone past it," he told her flatly.

"I guess it's a good thing you found me," she said, forcing a light tone she didn't really feel.

Colleen accepted the soup mug he handed her. The warmth pouring out of the little stove was starting to sink into her bones. She closed her eyes as she sipped the hot soup, savoring the taste of it, the heat of it. She thought it could be a long time before she felt completely warm again.

When she opened her eyes, she found Gun watching her, his expression unreadable. She laughed self-consciously. "I never realized how good chicken soup could taste."

"Hunger adds an edge." Her tongue came out to catch a stray droplet of broth at the corner of her mouth and Gun looked away. He'd obviously been up here too long when a woman drinking a cup of soup was starting to look sexy. Especially this particular woman.

"Where's your gear?" he asked abruptly, wanting a distraction.

"Under about a foot and a half of snow by now." Colleen took another swallow of soup. "I knew if I made it here, there'd be supplies, and trying to carry everything would have just slowed me down."

Gun nodded. "When it quits snowing, I'll take you down the mountain and we'll dig up your stuff. This can't last long," he said, with more hope than certainty.

"Mmm." Colleen made a noncommittal noise as she drank her soup. As far as she was concerned, it was welcome to snow all it wanted. She was safe and warm and with Gun.

She finished the soup and cradled the empty mug between her hands for a moment, drawing the last bit of heat from it. Though she was warm all the way through now, the memory of bitter cold lingered like a shadow sitting behind her. It had been so close. If Gun hadn't found her... Colleen shook her head and pushed the thought aside. There was no sense thinking about what might have been. He had found her and she was fine.

She leaned down to set the cup on the floor next to the bed and caught her breath as pain tightened the muscles in her left leg. Well, almost fine, she amended, her fingers massaging the ache.

"Is your leg bothering you?"

"A little." Glancing up, she caught the flicker of guilt in his eyes and moved her hand away from her leg as if the ache had been momentary and was already gone.

"Does it bother you much?"

"Only when I hike straight up a mountain in the middle of a blizzard," she said lightly. "Otherwise I don't even know it's there."

That wasn't entirely true. A shift in the weather could make the old injury ache, and it didn't take climbing up a mountain to remind her of the weakness there, but she didn't like the look in Gun's eyes, especially since she knew that she was responsible for the guilt he felt. If she hadn't lashed out at him, hadn't blamed him . . .

"It wasn't your fault, you know," she offered.

Gun had been sliding another chunk of wood into the stove and he finished the task, carefully latching the door before he turned to look at her.

"I was supposed to take care of you."

"You did. If you hadn't gotten me home, I probably would have died from exposure."

"If I hadn't let you go out, your horse wouldn't have fallen in the first place," he said, not giving an inch.

"*Let* me go out?" Colleen arched one brow, questioning the phrase. "I would have gone out riding that day, with or without you, Gun. You offered to go with me when Kel said he didn't want me to go alone. I don't see how you think you could have prevented Spooky from falling."

The accident had resulted in the death of her beloved horse and permanent injury to her own leg. It had been Gun who'd bound her leg and managed to get her onto his own horse and back to the ranch. And it had been Gun who'd borne the brunt of her hurt and anger when she'd lashed out, blaming him for her injuries and for the loss of her horse.

When the shock had worn off and she'd had time to think, she'd been ashamed of her reaction. Since she couldn't find the words to apologize, she'd taken the childish way out and had done her best to avoid Gun.

It had been her sister-in-law, Megan, who'd gently pointed out that, by avoiding Gun, she was reinforcing the impression that she blamed him for what had happened. With Megan's encouragement, she'd found the courage to apologize to Gun, to tell him that she didn't blame him.

"It wasn't your fault, Gun," she said firmly.

"Maybe not." Gun's broad shoulders lifted in a shrug and Colleen gave up the argument. Gun Larsen was the kind of man who took his responsibilities seriously. From his point of view, he'd failed to take care of her. No amount of logic could absolve him of responsibility in his own mind.

With a sigh, she leaned back against the pillows. She blinked sleepily. She would have liked to take a nap, but she knew Gun wouldn't let her. He'd keep her awake until he could be sure her sleep was the result of natural tiredness and not the lingering effects of her hours out in the cold.

Forcing down a yawn, she let her eyes linger on Gun as he went to the window and looked out again. Past his shoulder, she could see the snow still coming down, big heavy flakes that looked as if they intended to stay around awhile.

Colleen's mouth curved in a smile.

By late afternoon, Gun had to light a lantern so that they could see. The snow continued to fall, with no hint of a break in the clouds above. Darkness came early but without drama. The sunlight, which had been weak at best, slipped away so gradually that it was a surprise to realize it was gone.

Gun opened a can of chili and put it on to heat before going out to check on his horse. When he came back in, his expression was grim.

"Snow's coming down as fast as ever and the wind is starting to kick up."

Colleen tried to look properly concerned. "Do we have plenty of food?"

"Yeah." He pulled off his coat and hung it next to the door before going over to the stove. He held his hands out to the warmth. "There's a good stack of wood on the back porch and there's feed in the stable for Satan."

"Then we should be all right." The look Gun shot her suggested that her tone had been a little too cheerful. She pulled her mouth into a serious line. "Maybe it will stop snowing tonight and we'll have a chinook tomorrow. At least we can hope."

He looked doubtful but didn't argue. Colleen only hoped he didn't notice that her fingers were crossed.

Dinner consisted of chili and plenty of crackers. Afterward, Colleen insisted on rinsing off their dishes in water heated on the stove. Since the cabin had no running water, the bathroom was a quaint little building a few yards in back of the cabin. A single trip in the bitter cold was enough to make Colleen decide that roughing it had its place but not in the middle of a freak spring blizzard.

By the time she got back to the cabin, she felt as if she'd just stumbled out of a deep freezer. Gun helped her out of his coat and urged her close to the stove.

"There's a chamber pot on the back porch," he told her irritably.

"I'd rather die," she said through chattering teeth.

"Of all the stupid female attitudes."

"In case you hadn't noticed, I *am* female. That means I get to have female attitudes, stupid and otherwise."

"I'd noticed." The words didn't sound particularly complimentary but Colleen wasn't complaining. It was enough that he'd noticed. He didn't have to like it.

Since Gun didn't seem to be in a conversational mood, Colleen contented herself with reading a year-old issue of a popular women's magazine, which must have been left in the cabin by her sister-in-law. She perused an article entitled "How to Show Your Man That You Want Him." But most of the suggestions seemed to involve candlelight and silk teddies. The candles she might have been able to come up with, but the fancy lingerie was out of the question. And as for some of the other suggestions, she didn't think Gun was ready for her to give him a full body massage. Not that she wouldn't like to give it a shot, she thought, stealing a surreptitious look at the body in question.

He was sitting at the table, hunched over a month-old newspaper, apparently engrossed in a crossword puzzle. A very nice body it was. Broad shouldered and muscular, tapered and bulged in all the right places. Colleen gave a soundless sigh and admitted to herself that if she hadn't wanted to marry him since she was eight, she would still want to jump his bones. The man was sinfully good-looking. His features were strong and even, and his eyes were a blue so clear it seemed as if she could simply fall into them.

"Have I got dirt on my chin?" Gun's question made her realize that the eyes she'd been admiring were looking directly at her, their expression quizzical.

"No. I was...just thinking...about something I read." She ducked her head behind the magazine, hoping he wouldn't notice that the red in her cheeks now rivaled the color of her hair.

Gun insisted that Colleen take the bed while he slept on the floor. He silenced her protest by pointing out that, with a sleeping bag and an air mattress, he'd be doing at least as well as she would with the thin mattress and old box spring.

Since there was nothing to keep them up, they went to bed early. Gun had thought that once the light was out and he wouldn't be able to actually see Colleen, he might be able to think of her as Kel's little sister, rather than an attractive woman who put thoughts in his head that had no business being there. And it might have worked.

"Gun?"

Her voice came out of the darkness just as he had almost convinced himself that he'd forgotten she was there.

"Yeah?"

"I didn't thank you."

"For what?" He deliberately made his tone gruff, not wanting to encourage conversation. There was something a little too intimate about lying in the dark, talking to her, something that made it easy to remember the silky smoothness of her skin and hard to remember just who she was.

"For saving my life. And don't tell me you didn't save my life."

Gun felt his mouth curve. She *did* know him, didn't she? "Okay, I won't."

"Thank you."

"You're welcome."

She was quiet and he sensed there was more she wanted to say. But if that was the case, she changed her mind.

"Good night, Gun."

"Good night, Colleen."

He heard the rustle of covers as she shifted position, settling back against the pillow. It was easier than he would have liked to picture her hair spread across the plain white linen—like fire against snow.

Snow. He resolutely dragged his thoughts away from the woman lying a few feet away and considered the weather. He'd nearly succeeded in blocking Colleen from his thoughts when she spoke again.

"Gun?"

He bit back a groan. Wasn't she ever going to go to sleep? "Yeah?"

"I've read that, in some cultures, when you save someone's life, you're responsible for them forever."

"Sounds like something somebody made up."

"Maybe. But I bet there are people who believe it."
There was a pause and then, "You know, I guess this
is really the second time you've saved my life. The first
time was when I hurt my leg. So that would make you
responsible for me twice over."

"Or maybe the second time cancels the first out, like
pulling petals off a daisy. I'm responsible. I'm responsible not."

He knew if he turned his head in her direction, he
would have been able to see Colleen's smile. But he
didn't want to look in her direction, didn't want to be
reminded of how little distance there was between
them.

"Based on that theory, then the next time you saved
my life, you'd be responsible again."

"How about you try staying out of trouble so I
don't have to save your life again." Despite the tension he felt, the teasing smile in her words made his
mouth curve.

"I'll do my best. Besides, now that I think about it,
this is really the *third* time you've saved my life."

"How do you figure?"

"The first time was when you carried me down off
that windmill when I was eight. Remember?"

"I remember. But I don't think that qualifies as
saving your life. If I hadn't been there, Kel would have
gotten you down."

"Yeah, but then he'd have drowned me in the stock
tank."

"He was about mad enough to do it," Gun agreed,
smiling into the darkness.

"So I guess you're responsible for me again, since this is an odd number." She finished the sentence with a yawn.

"Except that's all nonsense. Now go to sleep."

"Okay."

He heard her settle back against the pillows again and wished that when Kel's grandfather had built this cabin he'd had the foresight to put in a separate bedroom. And while he was wishing, he might as well wish for the snow to stop and the sun to come out tomorrow morning or even simpler, he could wish that Kel had never offered an open-ended invitation to him to use the cabin or that he hadn't decided that he needed some time alone to think.

He listened to Colleen's slow breathing as she fell asleep. But since none of those things were likely or possible, there was no telling how long the two of them were going to be snowed in together.

And that didn't bear thinking about.

Gun stared out the window at the snow. There was no wind howling at the cabin walls, nothing dramatic or spectacular, just that steady fall of pretty white flakes of frozen rain. It was already too deep for him to walk through without difficulty. If it stopped soon, his horse would be able to force a path. A man his size needed a big horse and Satan fit the bill. But even Satan would have a hard time breaking a trail through heavy snow carrying two people on his back. Maybe with just Colleen . . . But she didn't seem desperately anxious to get out of here.

He turned to look at her. She was sitting cross-legged on the bed, humming to herself as she dealt a hand of solitaire with the worn deck of cards he'd found. She had the covers pulled over her lap. Her sweater had dried overnight, but she was still wearing his shirt, and he couldn't help but notice that, on her, even flannel looked sexy. He scowled. What was wrong with him, thinking of Kel's little sister that way? But she didn't look like anybody's little sister. She looked like . . . temptation.

Gun's frown deepened and he turned back to the window, glaring at the weather. The snow remained unintimidated and Colleen continued to hum cheerfully at his back. How could she sound so content? Sitting there humming and playing cards as though she was on vacation. And she'd been humming that same damn tune for ten minutes. His eyes widened as he realized what the song was.

"Don't you think you could find a more appropriate tune? I don't think 'Let It Snow' is what we need."

Colleen glanced up from her cards as Gun turned from the window and frowned at her. "Sorry."

She looked down again, catching her lower lip in her teeth to hide a smile. The song seemed very appropriate to her. The longer it snowed, the more time they were going to spending together. If she was lucky, it could be as much as a couple of weeks.

Two weeks. Alone with Gun. Her smile took on an almost predatory edge. She'd waited years for a chance like this. If she couldn't make him see her as a woman in those two weeks, even without silk teddies and candlelight, then she didn't deserve to have him. It might take more than two weeks for him to fall in love with her, but she certainly ought to be able to get the process started. She refused to consider the possibility that he might not fall in love with her at all.

"Glaring at the snow isn't going to make it stop," she commented as she set a black queen on a red king. "I'll play you a game of poker."

Gun let the curtain drop and turned to look at her. "Last time I played poker with you, I lost five dollars."

"That was eight years ago and I haven't played much since then. I'll be lucky if I even remember the rules."

"We don't have any chips."

"There's a box of toothpicks. We can use those."

Gun hesitated. Something told him that he'd be better off keeping his distance from her, but in a twelve-foot-by-twelve-foot cabin, there wasn't much hope of that anyway. With a shrug, he got the box of toothpicks. Colleen was gathering up her unfinished solitaire game, but she waved one hand to indicate the foot of the bed. Gun started to suggest that they move their game to the table, but then he remembered that her legs were bare under the hem of his shirt. He sat on the foot of the bed, wanting to believe he was concerned with her getting chilled and knowing he was more concerned with the impact those slender legs would have on his peace of mind.

"Five-card stud, deuces and jacks wild," she said briskly.

"Lucky if you remember the rules, huh?" Gun's brows rose as he watched her shuffle the cards with the grace of a professional dealer.

"I think they might come back to me." She conjured up a shy smile and batted her lashes at him.

"I think I'm about to be fleeced," he muttered as she cascaded the cards from one hand to the other, tapped them into a neat deck and gestured for him to cut.

Chapter 3

Two hours later, he was down to his last five toothpicks. Colleen had arranged her winnings in neat piles, like tiny stacks of cordwood, on the blanket in front of her.

"Dealer has a lady showing," she announced in an impersonal tone. "Possible two of a kind against a possible flush."

Gun looked at the four cards lying faceup in front of him and then lifted the single card that lay facedown. It was still a ten of spades, which meant he had a pair of tens and nothing else. Other than the queen, Colleen didn't have anything showing that could beat a ten, unless she had a pair. He looked at her face, trying to gauge what her hole card might be. But he couldn't read anything in her expression. Damned if she didn't have the best poker face he'd ever seen.

Still holding the black ten, he tapped his middle finger impatiently against it. Colleen met his look, her green eyes guileless. Hah! If he'd learned one thing in the past two hours, it was not to trust that look. She gave him the same look whether she held four aces or a handful of junk.

"Problem?" she asked.

"Just wondering if you have anything to go with that queen."

"It'll cost you your last five toothpicks to find out."

Setting his jaw, Gun dropped his pathetic stash on the pile of toothpicks between them and then flipped over his card. "A pair of tens," he said tersely.

"Not bad." Colleen nodded agreeably. "But not good enough. Two ladies."

Gun scowled at the pair of queens in front of her. "You're a cardsharp."

"Don't whine," she cautioned, gathering up her winnings and arranging them in those neat little piles.

"I'm not whining. I'm stating a fact. What did you major in while you were at college? How to fleece innocent cowboys out of their toothpicks?"

"Very few universities offer courses in gambling," she said, biting her lower lip against the urge to grin. She began putting her toothpicks back in their box.

"Are you going to leave me without a single toothpick?" he asked, managing to sound as if she was denying him a life necessity.

"Well…" Colleen considered his indignant face and then looked at the box of toothpicks. "I suppose I could let you have a few. But I'd have to charge interest, of course."

"Interest! Not only are you a cardsharp, now you're a loan shark. We have ways of handling people like you."

"We do?" It was all Colleen could do to keep from giggling.

"That's right, ma'am." His drawl was suddenly thick enough to butter. "Here in the West, we don't cotton to folks with big-city notions."

"But do you polyester to them?"

"We got our own way of handling things," he continued ominously, ignoring her facetious interruption.

"Wh-what kind of ways?" Suppressed laughter made her voice shaky.

"There's hangin'." He drew the word out as he leaned toward her.

"Over toothpicks?" Colleen's voice rose scornfully.

"It ain't the toothpicks, though I'd gotten kind of fond of the little critters," he added, casting a mournful look in the direction of the box. "It's the principle of the thing. I reckon hangin' is too good for a toothpick hustlin' woman like you."

"Toothpick hustler?" She could barely get the words past the laughter in her throat.

"Your kind requires strong measures."

"What kind of measures?" She caught the gleam in his eyes and held out one hand in a warding gesture. "Don't you dare. Gun!"

His name was a shriek of protesting laughter as he lunged toward her, his fingers finding the tender skin along her ribs and tickling mercilessly. During the laughing struggle that followed, the storm was forgotten. For a few minutes, they were both swept back ten years to when Colleen was a child and they'd wrestled playfully.

But this tussle wasn't destined to end as those so often had, with Gun holding her by her ankles and threatening to drop her on her head while she laughed and begged for mercy. The distance between then and now was suddenly brought vividly home to both of them when Colleen twisted, trying to slide out of his reach. Laughing, Gun grabbed for her, but she shifted at the last minute and, instead of his hand landing on her waist, his fingers closed over the soft curve of her breast.

The laughter was gone as if it had never been and in its place was the awareness Gun had been trying so hard to deny. Colleen's eyes, wide and startled, jerked to his face. For the space of several heartbeats, Gun couldn't move. He was vividly aware of the warmth of her skin under the thick flannel of his shirt, of the yielding weight of her flesh against his palm.

Hunger surged in him, thick and demanding. He was suddenly aware that she was sprawled on the bed beneath him, with only the blanket between them. Her hair was scattered across the pillows under her head, a skein of auburn silk against the stark white cotton.

He saw her eyes darken, felt a subtle softening of her slender body and knew he wasn't alone in what he felt. His gaze dropped to her mouth and her tongue came out and flicked over her lower lip in a quick nervous gesture. The sheen of moisture left behind seemed a blatant invitation to taste the softness of her mouth.

His head dipped.

Her lips parted.

With an oath, Gun rolled from the bed, his feet hitting the floor with a thud. He stood with his back to her for a moment, one hand gripping the nape of his neck as he struggled with the appalling realization that he'd been on the verge of kissing Colleen Bryan.

He heard the box spring squeak as she sat up behind him and sensed more than heard the quiet rustle as she straightened her clothes. What the hell was he supposed to say now? She had to know he'd been on the verge of kissing her.

"The toothpicks spilled on the floor," she said.

"What?" Gun turned to look at her, wondering if he'd imagined her words.

"The toothpicks," she repeated, sounding as cool and calm as if the past few minutes hadn't happened. "The ones you lost to me. They're all over the floor."

Gun followed her gesture and saw that the toothpicks were scattered at his feet. He swallowed, the apology he'd been about to offer suddenly stuck in his throat. Maybe he'd been wrong about the awareness he'd thought was in her eyes. Maybe he'd been about to make a fool of himself for apologizing for something that required no apology. After all, they were both adults here. His mouth twisted ruefully as he considered the vivid proof he'd just had of that.

"I'll get them." He crouched on the floor and began picking up the toothpicks.

Colleen drew her knees up to her chest and wrapped her arms around them. She was trembling. Not outside where Gun could have seen but deep inside where she could feel it all the way to her soul.

He'd been a heartbeat away from kissing her. Another second and he would have. She'd seen it in his eyes. For a moment, at least, he hadn't been seeing Kel's little sister or the child she'd been. He'd seen her as a woman. And he'd wanted her. She could feel the imprint of his hand on her skin, as if branded there. Her breast felt achy and swollen. Had he felt the way her nipple tightened against his palm? If he had, he must have known that she would have welcomed his kiss.

She tightened her arms around her knees and looked at him from under her lashes. He was so close. She had only to stretch out her hand to be able to bury her fingers in the thick gold of his hair. The hard set of his jaw kept her from giving in to that temptation. Gun might have wanted her but he didn't like it. She'd better give him some time to get used to the idea.

Colleen set her chin on her knees, her mouth curving softly. A little time, a little patience and Gun was going to figure out that they were made for each other. The patience was hers and the time was a gift of the weather. The longer it snowed, the more time she'd have with him.

Gun glanced at Colleen as he dropped the last of the toothpicks in the box. She was staring out the window at the snow and the dreamy look on her face made him uneasy. But not nearly as uneasy as the awareness he now felt when he looked at her. His palm seemed to tingle from the weight of her breast. And he could almost taste the warmth of her mouth.

Disgusted with himself, Gun stood and strode over to the stove. Pulling open the door, he tossed the toothpicks in, box and all. The bed of coals flared, flames licking up to devour this new fuel. Gun watched as the cardboard seemed to melt and the toothpicks burned.

It was too late to do it today, but first thing tomorrow morning he was going to dig out the radio that was kept in the cabin for use in emergencies and he was going to call Kel to come get his baby sister. Storm or no storm, he couldn't spend any more time alone in this cabin with Colleen.

Gun closed the stove door, his mind made up.

"Please don't tell Kel I'm here. You know what he'll do."

"He'll send someone up on a snowmobile to get you," Gun said, avoiding her pleading look.

"That's right and I don't want to go."

"The snow has stopped." He stirred water into a bowl of dehydrated eggs. "It's too deep for walking out, but a snowmobile won't have any trouble."

"But I don't want to go," she said again.

"You can't stay here." Not if he wanted to retain his sanity. Not to mention wanting to avoid the possibility of having his best friend murder him.

"Why not?" Colleen leaned across the table, forcing him to look at her. "I won't be any trouble."

You're already trouble.

"I'll do all the cooking."

"You're a lousy cook."

"I am not."

"I nearly broke a tooth on the biscuits you made that time you cooked dinner for Kel and me."

"That was *ten* years ago. I've learned a lot since then. I spent six months at the Culinary Institute in New York."

"What for?" Gun poured the eggs into a cast-iron skillet and set it on the stove.

"I thought I wanted to be a chef." She waved one hand impatiently, dismissing her culinary aspirations. "It doesn't matter now except that I'm a good cook."

"I won't starve to death on my own." He was doing his best to ignore the pleading look on her face. Dammit, it was for her own good that he wanted someone to come and get her. "Besides, why would you want to stay marooned up here, anyway?"

"If I go home now, I'm going to have to tell Kel that I quit school. Again."

"Again?" Gun turned to look at her, raising his brows in question. "How many does this make?"

"Not that many," she said with dignity.

"Seems to me it must be four or five at least."

"What difference does it make?"

"Not much, I guess." He turned back to the eggs and gave them a final stir before carrying the pan to the table and dumping them on the plates waiting there. Some fried corned-beef hash completed their breakfast.

"If I go home, Kel's going to give me that look." Colleen's gloomy tone matched her expression as she pushed the pile of eggs around the plate with her fork.

"What look?"

"That resigned look. The one that makes me feel like an idiot."

"Kel adores you and he doesn't think you're an idiot."

"I know that. But he doesn't understand why I can't stick with something long enough to graduate. I don't think he'd care what I graduated in, just as long as I graduate in something."

"So why don't you?" Gun took a swallow of coffee and looked at her down-bent head, trying not to feel sympathy for her.

"I don't know. I just haven't found what I want to do, I guess. I really thought I wanted everything I started out to study." She looked at him, her big green eyes earnest.

"You really *wanted* to be an accountant?" His arched brow emphasized the question.

"Well..." She dragged the word out and then wrinkled her nose as she shook her head. "I can't say I had a burning desire for that one, but I'd just quit art school and I thought maybe I should do something very practical. But I hated all those numbers."

"Not a good omen for your future as a CPA."

"No." She sighed and began arranging her eggs in a neat circle around the hash. "I liked English. I might have gotten a degree in that."

"Why didn't you?"

"Do you know what kinds of jobs you can get with an English degree?"

"Teaching?" he guessed.

"That's about it. I like kids but I don't want to teach." She began chopping the hash into tiny pieces with the side of her fork.

"What about the cooking school?" Gun pushed his empty plate away and leaned over to snag the coffee-pot from the stove, topping off both their cups.

"I liked that, but there isn't much call for highly trained chefs in Wyoming or anywhere besides a city. And one thing I learned while I was in New York is that I don't want to live in a big city."

"You could probably get work in Jackson Hole. Lot of money there these days."

"I suppose, but I just didn't *feel* like a chef."

"What does a chef feel like?"

"I don't know but I wasn't it." She was chopping the hash into smaller and smaller bits, being careful to avoid mixing it with the eggs she'd yet to touch.

"You're going to have to talk to Kel sooner or later," Gun said, stating the obvious. He wasn't going to feel sorry for her. Or if he did, he wasn't going to change his mind about getting her out of this cabin, out of his sight.

"I know I'm going to have to talk to Kel and tell him that I'm not going back to school, but I just wanted a few days to think about it before I talked to him. I need some time to figure out just what I want to do with my life." She glanced up, her mouth twisted in a self-deprecating smile. "There's got to be something I can stick with. I'm tired of drifting."

Tired of drifting. The words struck an echoing chord in him. He'd been doing just that for over twenty years and he was weary all the way to his soul.

"You could always go home." That choice wasn't open to him. Home was closed to him.

"I know. Kel and Megan have both told me that, but that's not what I want. The Lazy B Ranch is Kel's, not mine. I want something that's mine, something I can look at and say, 'I did that.'"

There was a long silence. Gun took a swallow of coffee and told himself that it didn't matter. She couldn't stay here. For her sake and his sanity, she definitely couldn't stay here.

"There's not enough room in this cabin to swing a cat."

"We've done okay the past couple of days."

Looking in her eyes, he saw no memory of the incident after their card game the day before. Maybe he was making too much of that. Maybe he'd imagined the spark that had seemed to arc between them.

"I came up here to be alone." He tried to sound unwelcoming, but he could feel himself weakening beneath the look in her eyes.

"You wouldn't even know I was here," she promised.

Not know she was here? God, he couldn't breathe without drawing in the scent of her.

"There's nothing to do. No TV, no radio, no nightlife."

"I came up here to camp, not to party," she reminded him. "Please, Gun. I really need this."

He needed it like he needed another hole in his head but he couldn't stand firm against the plea in her eyes. Not when he understood her need so well.

"All right. I won't radio Kel to come get you." He pushed his chair back from the table and grabbed his coat off the nail by the door. "I'm going to clear a path to the stable and check on Satan."

It wasn't exactly a gracious invitation to stay, Colleen thought as the door swung shut behind him. But it would do. She'd told him nothing more than the truth. She *did* need time to think, time to figure out where her life was headed. She was twenty-four years old, it was more than time for her to figure out what she wanted to do with her life.

The only time she was truly content was when she was home with Kel and Megan and her nephew, Michael. But as she'd told Gun, the ranch was Kel's, not hers, and she wanted—*needed*—to feel as if she was doing something that was hers alone.

Well, she had the thinking time she wanted and, as a bonus, she had time with Gun. She hoped to use both wisely.

Chapter 4

Four days after he'd agreed to let Colleen stay in the cabin, Gun was feeling a little foolish for having thought it might be a problem. She'd been everything she'd promised—quiet, unobtrusive and she really could cook. Obviously the days when her biscuits could have been used as weapons were long past.

Gun pulled open the stall door, automatically dodging Satan's halfhearted attempt to kick him.

"You're slowing down," he said as he nudged the big horse to the side of the stall. "Must be mellowing in your old age."

Satan rolled his eyes in Gun's direction. Gun recognized the look and rapped one knuckle firmly against the gray's nose. "You bite me and I'll send you to the glue factory. Damned if I know why I keep you. I've seen rattlesnakes with better tempers."

It was an old complaint and an old threat and neither one of them paid much attention. Satan had earned his name early in his career, along with a reputation for having crippled one cowboy and injured quite a few more. He'd been on the verge of being sold for dog food when Gun had bought him. There'd been no logic to it, since, until that moment, his only other significant possession had been a twenty-five-year-old Corvette. He hadn't known what he was going to do with a horse and couldn't have said just why he'd decided to save Satan from a fate he surely had earned.

He'd brought Satan back to the Lazy B, the closest he'd had to a home for the past twenty-four years. Kel had taken one look at the evil gleam in the big gray's eyes, told Gun he was crazy and asked what he wanted on his headstone. Some horses, like some people, just weren't meant to be social animals.

Gun had spent that whole summer working with Satan, and by the end of it, he felt they'd come to something of an understanding. Three years later Satan still didn't like Gun, but he'd tolerate him—most of the time. For Gun's part, he knew Satan kept an eye out for a chance to bite or kick, but he wasn't determined about it and he'd never had a horse with more stamina or sheer stubbornness when it came to going after a balky cow. He liked to think they shared an understanding, if not affection.

He poured some grain into the trough, keeping a watchful eye on Satan's teeth. But this morning it seemed, the big gray was more interested in breakfast than in testing to see who was in charge. Gun patted him on the rump on the way out of the stall. Later today he'd move Satan into the other stall and muck out the one he'd been using.

Gun stopped in the doorway and frowned at the pristine white landscape. Except for the pathway he'd forged between the cabin and the little stable, the snow was untouched and dazzling in its beauty. It was a scene out of a picture book. The picturesque log cabin with a pale curtain of smoke drifting up from the chimney, the white blanket of snow and the deep green of the pines for background.

Where was a little mud when you needed it, he thought, knowing he wasn't likely to see mud for days yet, not unless the thermometer made an abrupt shift upward. They hadn't had any new snow, but the temperature hadn't climbed much above thirty since the storm had ended.

The peaceful scene was a contrast to his troubled thoughts, which centered, as it seemed they always did lately, around Colleen.

It wasn't that Colleen had been any trouble. It was just that he didn't think the two of them staying alone together was a good idea. No matter how hard he tried, he couldn't quite erase the memory of how she'd felt sprawled on the bed beneath him, of the yielding weight of her breast in his hand. And every time he remembered it, it stirred thoughts he had no business having, at least not about Colleen Bryan.

It was getting harder and harder to think of her as Kel's little sister. She didn't look like anybody's little sister. What she looked like was pure temptation. He'd

never have believed that a flannel shirt about ten sizes
too large could be as sexy as chiffon and lace. But
somehow, when Colleen put it on, his shirt looked
downright risqué.

He'd been spending too much time alone. That was
the problem. As soon as the snow melted enough to
get down off this mountain, he was going to take Colleen home and then he was going to go to the nearest
town and find himself some company, preferably female, willing and unrelated to his best friend.

Still frowning, Gun stepped outside, turning to pull
the stable door closed behind him. He turned and
started toward the cabin and then stumbled back, a
startled oath escaping him as something struck him
solidly in the middle of the chest. He stared down at
the snow dusting the front of his coat and then lifted
his head to see Colleen looking around the corner of
the cabin at him. She must have crept along the edge
of the wall to avoid leaving footprints in the snow,
concealed herself along the side of the house and then
chosen her moment to launch a sneak attack.

"Looks like you got in the way of my snowball,"
she said, widening her eyes innocently.

"I suppose you weren't throwing it at me?" He used
the side of his hand to scrape the snow from his coat.

"Of course not. I just thought it was time to clear a
little of the snow away from the cabin." She took a
careful step back as he bent to scoop up a handful of
snow.

"You were going to clear the snow one snowball at a time?" He began packing the snow between his hands as he walked toward her.

"The longest journey begins with the first step." She offered the quote in the pious tone of one delivering wisdom to a heathen.

"That's true." He smoothed the snowball, his eyes gleaming as he watched her back away.

"Turning the other cheek is a very good quality," she suggested hopefully, backing away along the side of the cabin.

"That's true." Gun stopped as if considering this idea.

"On the other hand, the best defense is a good offense." The second snowball hit his shoulder.

Colleen didn't wait to see the success of her efforts. She turned and ran. Or as close to running as was possible in the deep snow.

The battle that followed was fast and furious. Colleen threw more snowballs but Gun's aim was devastatingly accurate. Her speed balanced his accuracy, making them more or less even as they pelted each other with packed snow, laughing and shouting like a pair of children.

With his longer legs and greater strength, Gun could have ended the fight anytime, but he deliberately held back and slowed down, allowing Colleen to keep out of his reach, dodging the fusillade of snowballs she fired in his direction, getting off enough shots of his own to powder her coat with snow.

"You'll never take me alive, copper!" she shouted defiantly. She fired off two hastily packed missiles and then tried to turn and run. But her boots stuck in the snow and she overbalanced. She landed with a thud, flat on her back in the snow, which was not nearly as soft as it looked.

Gun's shout of laughter echoed in the clearing, only to fade when she didn't get up right away.

"Colleen?"

When she didn't answer, Gun felt a jolt of fear go through him. She could have hit her head on a rock when she fell. He started toward her, cursing the fact that the snow slowed him. She could have fractured her skull, and they were miles from a doctor, even if he could get her down off the mountain. There was the radio, he remembered with relief as he dropped to his knees beside her. He was tearing his gloves off while he tried to estimate how long it would take Kel to get a snowmobile up to them.

Please, God, don't let it be anything serious. He was praying as he reached for her, sliding his fingers gently under her head, terrified he was going to feel the damp warmth of her blood.

She moved so quickly, it took him a moment to register what was happening. And that moment was all the time she needed to plaster his face with the handful of snow she'd been holding next to her side.

"Gotcha!"

Gun jerked back so violently that he nearly toppled over backward. He blinked the melting snow from his eyes as Colleen scrambled away on her hands and knees, trying to get to her feet. Visions of concussions and fractured skulls were replaced by much more satisfying images of murder and mayhem. When he got his hands on her...

With a growl he lunged forward, catching her around the waist just as she'd almost succeeded in getting her feet under her. He dragged her to the ground, shrieking and struggling, and used his strength and the sheer weight of his body to pin her.

"I thought you'd cracked your stupid skull," he roared, glaring down at her.

"I didn't mean to scare you, but you shouldn't have laughed when I fell."

"You looked ridiculous."

"About as ridiculous as you looked when I shoved that snow in your face, I bet."

It was difficult to hold on to his anger with her eyes sparkling up at him, bright green and full of laughter. "I could have had a heart attack," he muttered.

"I learned CPR in nursing school."

"When did you go to nursing school?"

"After accounting and before cooking. Let me up."

"Are you going to behave?"

"Probably not," she admitted cheerfully. She twisted her hands experimentally, but he had them pinned firmly over her head, held easily in one hand. "The snow is cold, Gun." She thrust her lower lip out in a hint of a pout, trying for sympathy.

"It's pretty cold melting down my neck, too." He didn't look sympathetic. He looked vengeful.

"I didn't think you'd be a poor loser."

"I didn't know I'd lost." Using his free hand, he tugged the collar of her coat open. "I think it only fair that you should see just how cold the snow really is."

"I thought we were friends." She lowered her chin protectively, but he simply wrapped his hand around her hair and tilted her head back.

"Friends share things."

"Gun!" His name ended on a shriek as he lowered his head and buried his cold, wet face against the warm skin of her neck. It was like having an ice cube dropped down her back. The shock of it sent a shiver up her spine. Laughing, protesting, she arched wildly, trying to throw his weight from her. But he was determined to exact a full measure of revenge and held her easily, rubbing his icy face against her throat.

Afterward, Gun couldn't say just when the moment changed. They were wrestling like a pair of children and then, suddenly, something shifted and there was nothing childlike about the mood at all.

She smelled of soap and snow and some indefinable scent he could only label "woman." Her skin was soft, and the body crushed so intimately beneath his curved in all the right places. He still had his fingers wrapped in her hair, but his hold shifted subtly, became less confining, more caressing. An almost imperceptible shift of his head and his mouth was touching her throat, tasting the pulse that suddenly jumped at its base.

Madness. This was madness.

He lifted his head, intending to pull away from her, to end this insanity before it got started. She was looking up at him, her eyes heavy lidded and full of awareness.

He felt the softening of her body where it lay stretched beneath him in the snow, a subtle shifting to accommodate the harder planes and angles of his much-larger frame. He should get up, he told himself, almost mesmerized by the fullness of her lower lip. This was crazy.

"Gun." The single word sighed over his skin in an almost physical caress.

His head dipped, his mouth hovering a breath above hers, a part of him insisting that this couldn't be happening. But any chance he might have had of regaining control of the situation ended when Colleen lifted her head, closing the distance between them as her mouth touched his.

The light touch was like a jolt of electricity going through Gun. He felt the shock of it all the way to his soles. Hunger rose in him, a deep, irresistible tidal wave of need. His mouth hardened over hers as he took control of the kiss away from her.

There was little of the tentative exploration that usually accompanied a first kiss. It was as if they'd kissed a hundred times. The softness of her mouth, the warm yielding of her body, the taste of her, the feel of her hair in his hands—it all seemed familiar, a part of him.

Gun's tongue slid along the fullness of Colleen's lower lip, asking for—and receiving—an invitation to enter, to explore. Her tongue came up to twine with his, her hunger feeding his own. He'd released his hold

on her wrists and her hands lifted, fingers sinking into
the thick gold of his hair, her body arching closer as
the kiss deepened into raw need.

The cold was forgotten. The snow could have been
a feather mattress for all the notice either of them took
of it. Nothing mattered but each other. Like a pitch-
soaked piece of kindling that flames at the first touch
of a match, the hunger that had lain unacknowledged
between them for the past few days flared to life. The
heat they generated was so powerful that Gun was almost surprised they didn't melt the snow around them.

But at the moment, he wasn't thinking about anything but the softness of Colleen's mouth, the warmth
of her body, the taste and feel of her, the rightness of
what was happening.

Odd as it seemed, it was this last thought that
brought him to a realization of what he was doing.
Actually, not so much *what* as with whom.

Rightness?

Since when was kissing Colleen right?

He tried to shove the thought away but it refused to
disappear. It nagged at the back of his mind as he felt
Colleen's fingers sliding deeper into his hair, flexing
against his scalp like a cat kneading her paws. His
hand swept down her body, resenting the thick layers
of clothing that separated them.

Kel would shoot me like a rabid dog.

The thought of his friend joined the chorus building in Gun's head. Kel trusted him. Never mind that
Kel didn't even know that Colleen was within a hundred miles of here. If he knew, he'd expect his best

friend to look after her. And that wouldn't include groping her in a snowbank.

His hand slid under the hem of her coat and his fingers flattened against her bottom, feeling the warmth of her skin through the fabric of her jeans. Her legs shifted, parting to cradle his growing arousal against the most feminine part of her.

She was so close. He could almost feel the damp heat of her, feel her body opening to welcome him, to take him inside. He thrust his tongue into her mouth, withdrew and then thrust again in a blatant imitation of the more intimate act. Colleen moaned softly against his mouth and brought her knees up alongside his hips. They were as close as it was possible to get while still fully dressed. But that wasn't nearly close enough.

He could take her right here and now. He could pull open their clothes and bury himself in her, ease the ache that had been with him ever since he'd brought her in from the storm and undressed her.

The very strength of his hunger startled Gun into breaking off the kiss. He rested his forehead against Colleen's, hearing her ragged breathing as an echo of his own. He could feel her trembling beneath him, feel the hunger in her. So close. He could carry her into the cabin, strip the annoying layers of fabric away.

"No." The word was more a groan than a definitive statement. What was the matter with him? He couldn't remember the last time he'd felt like this, on the verge of losing control.

But suddenly he did remember the last time. It had been more than twenty years, but the memory was still sharp enough to bring him to his feet as if he'd been stung.

"Gun?" Colleen stared up at him, dazed by the abrupt change. The wool cap she'd bundled her hair into had disappeared sometime during their playful tussle and her hair tumbled across the snow. Fire and ice, Gun thought. Her eyes were dark, her cheeks flushed. There was a sleepy look of arousal about her that went straight to his gut. He knew that all he had to do was lift her in his arms and carry her into the cabin and they could finish what they'd started here in the snow.

"Get up." He didn't wait for her to move, afraid that if she lay there one more second, looking at him with that sleepy hunger in her green eyes, he'd lose his already tenuous control. He leaned down and wrapped his hands around her shoulders, pulling her to her feet. He released her the moment she was steady, jerking his hands back as if she were made of fire.

"Gun? What's wrong?"

What was wrong? What was wrong was that he still wanted her. She ran her tongue over her lower lip as if she could still taste him there, and it was all Gun could do to keep from snatching her back into his arms. He curled his fingers into his palms.

"It's cold," he said finally.

Colleen stared at him, apparently stunned into silence by this statement of the obvious.

"I don't want you to catch a chill," he added when she didn't respond.

"I . . . wasn't really feeling the cold." And that had to be the understatement of the year, she thought. She could still feel the heat generated by their embrace, though it was dissipating beneath the chill in Gun's eyes.

"We should go in," he said, ignoring her mild attempt at humor.

Without waiting for a response, he turned and walked away. Colleen stayed where she was for a moment, her eyes following him. Obviously Gun was unhappy about something. Bending to pick up her cap, she followed after him, her expression thoughtful.

Chapter 5

"That can't happen again." Gun threw his gloves in the general direction of the table, ignoring them when they hit the edge and fell to the floor. "It shouldn't have happened even once," he muttered angrily. "But it's not going to happen again."

Colleen unzipped her coat, moving slowly to conceal the fact that her fingers were not quite steady. In fact, she didn't think there was a steady muscle in her body. She felt as if she'd been picked up by a whirlwind, spun around and around and then set back down again. She hadn't quite regained her balance yet and she avoided looking at Gun as she took off her coat and hung it ever so carefully on a hook.

Ever since she was old enough to understand what kissing was all about, Colleen had fantasized about having Gun kiss her. Not the casual pecks on the cheek 'he'd occasionally given her when she was a child, but a real kiss, the kind a man gave a woman when he wanted her. She hadn't eschewed getting in a little practice while she waited and she'd thought kissing a very pleasant activity. But neither practice nor fantasy had prepared her for the impact of Gun's kiss. She wasn't sure her knees would ever feel quite steady again.

"Well?" Gun demanded impatiently when she didn't say anything.

"Well, what?" Colleen turned to look at him, her expression calm.

If the light had been better, he might have seen the stunned look in her eyes, might have realized that she wasn't nearly as calm as she appeared, but all he saw was that she seemed unmoved by something that had shaken him to his core. It was an infuriating thought. It made him want to grab her and shake her. Even worse, he wanted to kiss her again and keep on kissing her until she was trembling and unsteady.

Muttering an oath under his breath, he jammed his fingers through his hair and spun away from her. He'd lost his mind. That was the only possible explanation. It was bad enough that he'd done what he'd sworn he wouldn't do and kissed her, but all he could think of now was how much he wanted to do it again.

"That can't happen again," he said for the third time, wishing the words sounded less empty.

"Why not?" Colleen's calm question brought him back around to face her.

"Why not?" he repeated in disbelief.

"That's what I said." She met his incredulous look calmly. "Why not?"

"Because it can't," he snapped. He stalked to the stove and jerked the door open, stuffing several chunks of wood in on top of the glowing coals.

"I liked kissing you."

The bald statement caught him off guard. He grabbed the door handle, jerking his hand back with a startled oath when the hot metal burned his skin.

"Are you hurt?" Colleen was across the room in a heartbeat, grabbing his hand to check for burns.

For a moment, Gun was frozen. Her scent drifted up to him and the feel of her hand on his, innocent as it was, set off shock waves that were far from innocent. He snatched his hand back.

"I'm fine!" He slammed the stove door shut, this time remembering to use the rag that served as a pot holder. "What the hell did you mean by that?"

"By what?" Colleen faced him as calmly as if they were discussing the weather.

"Saying you liked kissing me." He made the words sound like an insult.

"I meant exactly what it sounds like. I liked—"

"I heard you the first time." He cut her off, afraid that if he heard her say it again he wasn't going to be able to resist the urge to grab her back into his arms and demonstrate that she wasn't the only one who'd liked it.

"Didn't you like it?" she asked, as if reading his mind.

"You're not that naive," he growled, giving her a look that made the stove beside her seem cool in comparison. She slid her hands into the back pockets of her jeans to conceal their trembling.

"Then I don't see what the problem is." She was proud of the even tone of her voice, but it didn't seem to do anything for Gun's temper.

He turned away from her and jammed his fingers through his hair again, ruffling it into thick golden waves that made her want to smooth them into place.

"Whether or not either one of us liked it is not the point," he said after a moment. It was obvious that he was struggling to sound cool and collected. "It's not going to happen again."

"Why not?"

"Would you stop asking that!" His voice was only marginally lower than a shout and the look he turned on her reflected the frazzled tone.

"I'll stop asking when you give me an answer." The words were steady, but she could feel her knees starting to shake with the effort it cost her to appear calm.

"An answer?" Gun glared at her. "You're too young for me. How's that for an answer?"

"Not very good. I'm twenty-four. You're forty. Sixteen years isn't exactly a lifetime. I'm hardly a child, Gun."

As if he needed a reminder of that, he thought savagely. He had only to let his eyes drop from her face to the ripe curves so invitingly hinted at by the loose flannel of his shirt to know that she was most definitely *not* a child.

"You're Kel's sister." It was the one unanswerable, insurmountable answer to her question.

"Being Kel's sister doesn't make me asexual. I'm a woman before I'm a sister. Having a brother doesn't prevent me from having sexual relations."

The phrase "sexual relations" immediately conjured up images of Colleen in another man's arms, in another man's bed. In this day and age, it was unlikely that she'd reached the age of twenty-four without having a lover, quite possibly more than one.

Gun had never been much of a believer in the double standard. As far as he was concerned, it was ridiculous to expect women to subscribe to a standard of behavior that men had been ignoring for centuries. At least, he'd always believed that until this minute. But the thought of Colleen with another man, any other man, made him want to do serious hurt to that man.

The violence of his reaction startled him. He wanted to believe it was just because this was Colleen, whom he'd watched grow up; that it was a brotherly kind of thing. But there was nothing brotherly about his feelings toward her. And if he'd still had any doubts about that, the kiss had erased them.

The kiss. That was what they were discussing, what he was supposed to be thinking about. Whether or not she'd had one or a hundred lovers was none of his business. With an effort, he dragged his mind back to the conversation at hand.

"Kel trusts me to take care of you," he said, bringing the discussion back to what was, as far as he was concerned, the central point.

"You have taken care of me. If it weren't for you, I'd be a human popsicle right now."

"That's not the point." It was damned hard to stick to the point when she was standing in front of him with her mouth still swollen from his kisses and all he could seem to think of was how much he wanted to kiss her again. "I don't think Kel would appreciate my fishing you out of a snowbank and then seducing you."

"I don't think it's any of Kel's business," she snapped, letting her annoyance show for the first time. "I'm a grown woman, Gun. I don't need my brother's permission to take a lover."

Lover. The word hung in the air between them as if painted in fiery letters. The images it conjured were powerful and vivid.

Gun stared at Colleen. For a moment, she saw a stark hunger in his eyes. She drew in a quick breath, her skin heating. And then the look was gone, his blue eyes taking on a steely gray edge.

"It can't happen again," he said flatly.

Colleen opened her mouth to continue the argument and then closed it again without speaking. The set of his jaw made it obvious that she'd be wasting her breath. Arguing with him now would only make him even more determined that he was right. She lifted her shoulders in a shrug, which he could interpret to mean anything he liked.

"I think I'll get supper started."

There was a moment's silence and she saw relief dawn in Gun's eyes. He nodded. "I'll go check on Satan."

Colleen could have pointed out that he'd checked on Satan not half an hour before, but she said nothing. She nodded and aimed a vague smile in his direction as she pulled open a cupboard door and tried to look as if she was engrossed in deciding whether to prepare canned chili and tamales or canned spaghetti for their supper.

The instant the door shut behind Gun, Colleen's calm pose dissolved. She closed her eyes and rested her forehead against the edge of the cupboard door. Her knees were steadier than they had been when she'd first walked into the cabin and her pulse had slowed to something approaching normal, but she still felt as if she'd just gotten off a wild carnival ride, one that had left her shaken and trembling.

He'd kissed her. *Finally*.

It seemed as if she'd spent most of her life waiting for it to happen and it finally had. And what a kiss! Still leaning against the cupboard door, Colleen grinned. If she'd ever thought the act of kissing a pleasant but slightly overrated activity, she'd just been proven wrong. Gun's kiss had done everything writers claimed a kiss could do. Her toes had curled, and her heart had been beating so fast she wondered if kissing shouldn't be added to the list of cardiovascular workouts. At least, kissing with the right man.

And Gun was most definitely the right man. She might have to work at convincing him of that fact, but as long as the weather continued to cooperate, she'd have a few more days to try. She'd just have to work on his ridiculous idea that being Kel's sister put her off-limits.

She frowned briefly, considering Kel's possible reaction to the news that she and Gun were intimately involved. Her teeth worried her lower lip. Though Kel was generally the most perfect of older brothers, she had to admit that there were times when he could be a little overprotective of her. It was possible, she admitted cautiously, that he wouldn't be wildly enthused about the idea at first.

But she couldn't spend time worrying about Kel's reaction, not when there was the memory of that incredible first kiss to relive. First kiss but not the last—not if she had anything to say about it. She wouldn't push too quickly. Gun wanted her and they both knew it. It was enough for now, she decided, smiling in a way that would have made Gun very nervous if he'd been there to see it.

Satan, perhaps taking pity on his owner's absent-minded mood, had neither bitten Gun nor kicked him, though he'd been presented with more than the usual opportunities for both. Gun ran the currycomb over the big gray gelding's coat, his thoughts back in the cabin.

He'd made himself clear. He'd left no room for doubt about how things were going to go from here on out. "It can't happen again," he'd told Colleen. Firmly.

It occurred to him now that the shrug she'd given as a response could be open to interpretation. He'd assumed it indicated acquiescence. But there'd never been anything particularly acquiescent about Colleen Bryan. Not the child he'd known, and not, he suspected, the woman she'd become.

Not that it mattered whether she'd been agreeing with him or not, he told himself. Because what had happened between them this afternoon wasn't going to happen again. He was positive of that.

Almost.

Four days after the snowball fight and its unexpected ending, the atmosphere in the small cabin was thick enough to cut with a knife. Half a dozen times, Gun considered radioing Kel to come and get his sister. He'd have done it in a minute if it hadn't been for the memory of the wistful look in her eyes when she'd told him about needing time to think, to try to find what she wanted to do with her life. It would have seemed like a betrayal to deny her that time.

Besides, it wasn't as if he could give her a good reason for going back on his promise. She seemed to have accepted his decision that nothing more than friendship was possible between them. Gun frowned at the piece of wood he was pretending to carve, his thoughts on the woman who lay on her stomach on the bed a few feet away, apparently engrossed in the tattered copy of *Tarzan of the Apes* that she'd unearthed from somewhere.

It wasn't her fault that the taste of her seemed to linger on his mouth. It wasn't her fault that the cabin was small enough to put them practically on top of each other.

Bad thought, he told himself as the analogy brought startlingly vivid images to mind. Images of Colleen lying on the narrow bed, his weight pressing her into the mattress, an even more provocative picture of her straddling his hips, her hair spilling like polished fire down her back, her breasts...

Gun swore as the knife he'd been using slipped and the blade sliced a shallow cut in the pad of his thumb.

"Are you okay?"

"Fine," he mumbled around the injured digit, which he'd stuck in his mouth.

"Do you need a bandage?" She started to sit up.

"No!" Colleen's eyebrows shot up at his violent response and Gun forced a smile. "It's just a scratch."

"Are you sure?"

"I'm sure." He was sure he didn't want her touching him. He felt about as volatile as a keg of gunpowder. He didn't need her lighting a match.

She shrugged and went back to her book. Since the cut on his finger had already stopped bleeding, Gun picked up the knife and the chunk of wood and tried to concentrate on his carving. But his attention soon wandered to the woman sprawled on the bed just a few feet away.

He was unreasonably irritated by her relaxed pose. She didn't seem to be having any trouble ignoring him.

So why the hell couldn't he get her out of his head? Why did it seem as if her scent was everywhere, clinging to his clothes, haunting him even when he slept?

Gun wanted to believe it was because of the past months of abstinence, but he couldn't convince himself that that was all it was. He'd been celibate for extended periods before and, while it might not be his favorite way to live, he'd never had a real problem with it. Twenty-four years ago he'd learned some hard lessons about letting his zipper rule his life. He'd never forgotten them, never wanted to forget them. Until now.

Colleen made him want to forget those lessons, forget that he was her brother's best friend, that she was too young for him, forget everything but the softness of her skin and the warmth of her mouth.

"Damn!" The oath escaped him as the razor-sharp blade extracted fresh vengeance for his inattention. He jerked his hand back, the piece of wood sailing from his grip.

"How bad is it?" Colleen sat up and swung her legs off the side of the bed.

"Not bad," he said quickly without bothering to look at the injury. "Just a scratch."

"Maybe you need something harder."

Gun's eyes shot to her face in startled question.

"The wood," she clarified, nodding to where the half-carved block lay beside the stove. "Maybe you need a harder piece of wood. Or a duller knife."

"Yeah." Gun returned her teasing smile with a halfhearted grin. What he needed was for the snow to melt so he could get the hell out of this cabin before he forgot all the reasons he shouldn't tumble her back on that bed and make passionate love to her.

He stood and grabbed a ragged towel from the tiny kitchen counter and dabbed the thin line of blood from his finger. This second cut was no more serious than the first. No hope that he'd bleed to death and put himself out of his misery, he thought with black humor.

Trying not to look at Colleen, who'd picked up her book again, he crossed to the stove to retrieve the half-finished and hopelessly bungled carving. Crouching down, he stretched his arm between the stove and the wood box to reach the carving. Just as his fingers closed around it, a flutter of white caught his attention.

Lifting his eyes, he looked past the squat black bulk of the stove to where two scraps of cotton knit were draped across a broom handle propped at an angle over the hearth. Colleen's underwear. She must have washed it out and hung it back there to dry. Gun drew his arm back, the carving forgotten in his hand, his eyes riveted on those modest bits of fabric. If Colleen's underwear was hanging behind the stove, that meant that she couldn't be wearing it.

Which meant she wasn't wearing anything beneath his shirt and her jeans.

His fingers tightened until the edge of the wood pressed painfully hard against his palm. He had to be out of his mind, kneeling here envying a damned shirt.

Standing up, he opened the stove door and tossed his botched artistic effort onto the bed of coals.

"I take it Rodin doesn't need to shiver in his grave," Colleen said.

"Not right away."

Though he knew it was a mistake, Gun couldn't keep his eyes from her. The shirt, which was modest by even the most puritanical of standards, was suddenly wildly erotic.

"Maybe you should try basket weaving." She smiled teasingly. "Or needlepoint."

"I don't think I'm the needlepoint type."

"If Rosie Greer can do it, I don't see why you couldn't."

"At the rate I'm going, I'd probably stab myself with a needle."

"I think needlepoint uses a dull needle," she commented. She stood and arched her back in a luxurious stretch. "I think I'll heat some water to wash up. I'm getting stiff from all this sitting."

Gun's eyes were riveted on the gentle sway of her unbound breasts. He was getting stiff, too, but the reasons had nothing to do with sitting and everything to do with her. He ached to slide his hands beneath the tails of the shirt, to feel the silky skin of her back, to cup the soft globes of her breasts.

"I'm going to muck out Satan's stall," he said abruptly.

She gave him a surprised look. "I thought you did that this morning."

"Maybe it needs to be done again." He snatched his coat off its hook and was opening the door even as he shrugged into it. "I may be a while," he said over his shoulder. A second later, the door banged shut behind him.

Chapter 6

Colleen's lower lip thrust out in a pout as the door shut behind him. What was she going to have to do to get him to notice her? She'd done everything but strip naked and throw herself at his feet and she was starting to seriously consider that as an option.

Her movements made jerky by irritation, she dipped the kettle into the bucket of water and set it on the stove to warm. He couldn't possibly be as unaware of her as he was pretending to be. Not after the way he'd kissed her four days ago. A man couldn't kiss a woman with all that fire and passion and then just turn it off like flicking off a light switch. Could he?

Colleen stared unseeingly at the kettle. What did she really know about what he could or couldn't do? With all the schooling she'd had in a wide assortment of subjects, she'd never learned anything that could have helped her handle this situation. Too bad there wasn't a class that taught a woman how to deal with a pig-headed cowboy who didn't want to admit what was right in front of his nose, which was that the two of them were perfect for each other.

She'd just have to learn on the job. She might not have had a whole lot of experience when it came to seduction, but all she needed was a basic understanding of biology to know that Gun had wanted her four days ago. If they hadn't been lying in the middle of a snowbank, things might have had a *very* different ending.

But then he'd started insisting it couldn't happen. She'd thought it would be fairly easy to change his mind about that, but he was proving more stubborn than she'd hoped. Without being obvious about it, she'd tried to make herself noticeable. It would have been nice if she'd had something more seductive than a pair of jeans and Gun's flannel shirts, but she'd done the best she could with what was at hand. Leaving an extra couple of buttons undone, brushing against him when she put food on the table. But so far, he was resisting her attempts at seduction. Either that or he didn't find her charms as irresistible as she'd hoped. What a depressing thought that was.

Colleen was frowning as she got out the chipped enamel bowl that served as a wash basin. The water in the kettle was steaming and she poured some of it into the bowl. A splash of cold water from the bucket was all that was needed to take the edge off the heat. She pinned her hair up with pins she'd had in her jeans pocket.

She unbuttoned the flannel shirt and slipped it off. Gun had said he was going to be a while, and he always knocked before he opened the door, so she had no hesitation about draping the shirt across the back of one of the chairs. Once she'd washed her upper body, she'd put the shirt back on, slip her jeans off and finish bathing. If her underwear was dry, she'd put it back on.

Dipping a thin washcloth in the water, she brought it to her face, savoring the warmth of it against her skin. Next time she got lost in a blizzard, she sincerely hoped that the nearest shelter came complete with hot and cold running water. There were times when she wasn't sure which she wanted more—Gun or a hot shower.

Smiling a little at the thought, Colleen ran the soapy washcloth down one arm, moving briskly. The homely little stove did a good job of heating the cabin, but the temperature wasn't balmy enough for her to linger over her makeshift bath.

She'd washed and dried her torso and had just stretched out one arm to snag her shirt from its resting place when the cabin door opened without warning and Gun stepped inside. She thought later that he must have been so preoccupied with his thoughts that he hadn't remembered to knock. But he was not so preoccupied that he didn't notice a half-naked woman standing in front of him. He came to an abrupt halt just inside the door, his eyes riveted on her.

"Gun!" His name came out on a squeak of surprise. Colleen snatched the shirt up and held it in front of her in a classic pose of modesty.

Time stood still.

He should turn around and walk right back out, Gun thought. He should apologize and leave. No big deal. They were both adults. Both adults. Wasn't that what he'd been trying to deny? That Colleen was an adult? But it certainly wasn't a little girl standing in front of him right now.

He was going to leave any minute now, he told himself. Any minute. An absent flick of his hand shut the door, closing the two of them inside the little cabin. Closing out the world. His gaze raked over her, taking in the tousled bun that held her hair and the bare curves of her shoulders. He wasn't going to let himself forget all the reasons to keep his distance from her. Just because she was the most desirable woman he'd ever seen, that didn't mean he was going to forget. Just because the blood was heating in his veins and his jeans were suddenly much too tight, that didn't mean anything had changed. There were still reasons... even if he was having a hard time remembering what they were.

Colleen could feel the conflict in him, the struggle between what he wanted and what he thought was right. The blatant desire in his eyes was almost as potent as a touch. She hesitated, her fingers tightening over the bunched fabric of his shirt until the knuckles turned white. If she hadn't spent her whole life wanting him, if there'd been any real reason they should keep their distance, she wouldn't have made the choice she did.

She boldly dropped her arms to her sides, letting the shirt slide from her fingers. Naked to the waist, she faced him. Her chin tilted with challenge even as the color climbed in her cheeks. She waited for Gun's reaction.

Gun stared at her, feeling hunger slam through him. He'd spent days trying not to imagine her like this, but his imagination could never have come close to the reality. His eyes devoured her, tracing every curve and indentation, even as he told himself it was wrong, that he should walk away.

The moment stretched, a silence broken only by the muffled popping of the fire inside the stove. Just when Colleen was convinced that she'd accomplished nothing more than her own utter humiliation, Gun's eyes lifted to her face. The blatant hunger in his look stole her breath and weakened her already shaky knees.

Without saying a word, he jerked his gloves off, letting them fall to the floor. An instant later, his coat joined them. And a heartbeat after that, he was standing in front of her, his hands cupping her face, tilting it up to his. With a sob that was part relief, part need, Colleen melted against him.

The tension that had been between them since her arrival snapped at the first touch of his mouth on hers. He devoured her, his tongue diving into her mouth, tasting the heat of her response. There was no need for a slow build to passion and no time for it. The hunger had been denied too long to allow for patience.

If his fingers were impatient with the snap on her jeans, hers were just as impatient with the buttons on his shirt. He succeeded in lowering her zipper just as she managed the last button and pulled open his shirt. His hands slid up her sides. Colleen sucked in her breath as his thumbs brushed across the peaks of her breasts. Every nerve in her body was suddenly, achingly alive, stretched taut with need.

His mouth was hot against her throat, his tongue finding the pulse at its base and sending it rocketing. His hands left her breasts, sliding across the smooth skin of her back and beneath the loosened fabric of her jeans to cup her bottom. Colleen gasped in surprise as her feet left the floor. She grabbed automatically for his shoulders as he lifted her until her breasts were at eye level.

She closed her eyes, her heart pounding with anticipation. But when the moment stretched and he still hadn't touched her, she opened her eyes again and tilted her head to look at him. He was simply looking at her, his eyes tracing over her breasts. She felt that look as if it were a touch, her nipples tightening and hardening, her skin becoming exquisitely sensitive.

Just when she thought she'd die if he didn't touch her, he leaned forward and flicked his tongue across one swollen bud. The sensation was so intense it bordered on pain, and then he took her fully into his mouth and Colleen felt the world rock. Gun took his time, savoring every tender curve, every sweet inch of her, with his mouth and tongue. Held suspended between heaven and earth, she was helpless to do anything but feel.

By the time he lowered her to the floor, her legs were trembling so badly that they refused to support her and she had to cling to the sides of his shirt for support. Gun gave her no time to recover her balance but swept her up in his arms and carried her to the narrow bed where she'd slept alone, dreaming of him.

The old box spring creaked a protest as it took their combined weight. Gun struggled to strip Colleen's jeans down her long legs, his hands impatient. Always before, he'd prided himself on his control, on his ability to draw the moment out. But he felt none of that control now. His pulse pounded in his ears, deafening him to the small voice inside that questioned his urgency.

Colleen's hands were equally impatient with his clothes, yanking the open shirt from his shoulders. Later, there'd be time for all the things they were rushing past. Later, there'd be time for soft touches and softer sighs, for whispers and gentle caresses. But now they were driven by a need that couldn't be denied, by an urgency that couldn't be slowed.

The narrowness of the bed had Gun cursing under his breath as he struggled with their clothes. At another time, he might have seen the humor in the situation, might have even let laughter drift into passion. But with the blood drumming in his ears, all he could think of was that he had to touch Colleen, had to feel her skin under his hands—now.

With a low sound that was more a growl than a word, he rose, dragging her to her feet, holding her there as he stripped the stubborn denim from her. Her jeans hit the opposite wall with a muffled thud before falling to the floor.

Looking at her, he went absolutely still, and for all her boldness earlier Colleen suddenly felt self-conscious. She half lifted her hands as if to cover herself and then let them drop to her sides, realizing how ridiculous the gesture would seem.

"You are so beautiful." They were the first words either of them had spoken since he'd walked into the cabin and surprised her. "So incredibly beautiful. Perfect."

Colleen flushed beneath the look in his eyes. She'd never considered herself more than reasonably pretty, but the way he was looking at her, the desire in his eyes, made her feel beautiful.

"Aren't...aren't you overdressed?" Her voice was little more than a whisper, her earlier daring washed away by the newness of what she was feeling.

In response, Gun's hands dropped to the waist of his jeans. She looked away, suddenly shy as she listened to the rasp of his zipper, then the sound of the denim sliding over his skin. She heard his jeans hit the floor and then silence. He waited, letting the seconds tick away until she finally couldn't resist looking. She was struck dumb by the sheer masculine beauty of him.

Her eyes took in the thick muscles that corded his arms and shoulders. A dark gold mat of hair covered his chest, narrowing into a thin line that cut across the flatness of his stomach before thickening again across his loins. Her eyes touched on his arousal and then veered away, skimming over the muscled length of his legs before being drawn again to the unmistakable evidence of his desire.

Gun saw the uncertainty in her face and made a last-ditch effort to grab hold of his sanity. But before he had a chance to remind himself of all the reasons this shouldn't be happening, Colleen's hand came out, her fingers tentative as she touched him. He groaned and caught her wrist in his hand.

"Did I hurt you?" She looked at him, her eyes startled.

"No. Yes." He closed his eyes, conscience and desire waging a last fierce battle. "This is crazy," he said, opening his eyes again and looking at her. "I should stop it before it's too late."

"Don't you want me?" Her fingers shifted deliberately and Gun couldn't bring himself to stop her as she closed her hand over him.

Sweet torture.

"I think you know the answer to that," he managed to say through his teeth.

"And I want you," she whispered, letting her fingers explore the turgid length of his erection. "There's nothing stopping us."

Nothing but my conscience and it doesn't seem to be working too well at the moment.

Gun brought his hand up, threading his fingers through her hair as he dragged her up against him, his mouth closing over hers in a kiss that was part anger, part frustration and pure hunger.

The world spun around her and it wasn't until Colleen felt the bed come up under her that she realized the feeling was based at least partially on fact. She moaned as Gun's body came down over hers, one leg sliding heavily between hers.

His hand swept down her body, fingers threading through the fiery triangle of curls that covered her femininity. At his touch, she gasped, her slender body stiffening as if in shock and then she seemed to melt against him, her hips arching into his hand.

Gun fought the urge to give her what she was asking for, to bury himself in her welcoming body, to find surcease for his aching desire. Something was nagging at him, tugging at the edges of his thoughts, demanding his attention. He cupped his hand over her hip, stilling her restless movements, even as she whimpered with hunger.

"Are you protected?" he asked, his voice raspy.

"Protected?" She stared at him, her eyes drugged with need. "From what?"

"Birth control," he clarified, struggling to ignore the dampness of her against his fingers.

She shook her head. "It doesn't matter."

"You could get pregnant." It was so hard to think clearly. He could smell the musky scent of her arousal, feel her hunger echoed in the thrumming of his pulse.

"It's a safe time of the month for me," she said, having no idea if it were true and caring less. She saw the doubt in his eyes and reached between them to close her fingers over his arousal, feeling the shudder that ran through him at her touch.

"Would it be so terrible?" she whispered, stroking him. "Would it be so terrible if I had your baby?"

Gun was stunned into silence by the question, even more stunned by the wave of longing that swept over him at the thought of her carrying his child. He'd given up the idea of having a family years ago, telling himself it was enough to be a kind of adoptive uncle to his friends' children. But he suddenly ached to hold a child of his own, have a son or daughter to love.

It was insane. Madness. There was no justification, no way to rationalize what he was about to do. There'd be regrets and recriminations later. It was wrong. But something stronger than himself was whispering how right it was.

"I don't know which one of us is crazier," he whispered, easing his hips between her parted thighs.

"Who cares?"

Gun had no answer. He felt the slick heat of her against his arousal and knew that, whether it made any sense or not, nothing had ever felt so right in his entire life. He heard Colleen suck in a quick breath as he eased inside the damp sheath of her body and forced down the urge to thrust home. He knew his size could be intimidating, and much as he wanted to find his own release he wanted her with him every step of the way.

With a wordless murmur of reassurance, he pressed deeper. Beads of sweat popped out on his forehead. She was so incredibly tight, almost as if...as if she'd never done this before. Gun lifted his head, staring down at her in shocked question.

"Colleen?" Her name was all he could get out, but she seemed to know what he was asking.

"Don't stop," she whispered urgently. Her fingers dug into his hips as if to hold him to her. "Please, Gun. Don't stop now."

"As if I could." His voice rasped in his throat as he completed their joining.

Colleen held herself very still, trying to adjust to the reality of sharing her body with a man. She'd thought she knew what to expect, that there was no real mystery to the act. But nothing she'd ever read or seen had prepared her for the incredible feeling of her body stretching to accommodate Gun. Or for the almost painful intimacy of the act.

She gasped as he eased back and then slowly thrust forward again. Murmuring encouragement, he repeated the movement until her body began to echo his. Sensation lapped outward from where they were joined. Colleen began to tremble, half-frightened by the intensity of it. It was as if a spring coiled inside her, drawing tighter and tighter until her entire being was concentrated on those coils. It was too much and yet he continued to drive her higher.

Her breath rasping in her throat, Colleen arched against him, almost fighting him, though she couldn't have said what she was fighting for. She needed something...something that lay just beyond her reach.

And then Gun's hand slid between them, touching her just above their joining and the tension inside suddenly shattered in a thousand glittering shards of sensation. Her short nails dug into his muscled back, her entire body going rigid beneath him. She felt Gun shudder as her body tightened around his, then heard his guttural groan as her climax triggered the powerful pulse of his own release. Linked, body and soul, they tumbled headlong into pleasure.

It was several minutes before Gun gathered the strength to move. Colleen murmured a protest, her hands clinging to him.

"I'm not going far," he promised, easing his weight from her. Unless he got out of bed, he *couldn't* go far. And he had no intention of getting out of bed. In for a penny, in for a pound, he thought ruefully as he slid his arm under Colleen's shoulders and settled her against his body. The time for trying to keep his distance from her was past.

"Are you all right?" His fingers under her chin tilted her face up to his, his eyes searching.

"I'm better than all right." Her smile held a sensual innocence that made him catch his breath.

"Why didn't you tell me it was your first time?" He brushed the hair back from her forehead, feeling it curl around his fingers.

"Because you'd have stopped and I didn't want you to."

"I should have stopped." He frowned, his conscience stirring uncomfortably.

"No regrets." Colleen reached up to stroke her fingers over the lines on his forehead. "I'm not a child, Gun. I knew exactly what I was doing."

"No, you're definitely not a child." He couldn't resist the urge to stroke his hand down her back. She arched like a cat. The movement pressed her breasts more firmly against his chest in a graphic demonstration of just how unchildlike she was. But that didn't mean he'd been any less wrong....

"No regrets," she said again, reading his thoughts in the troubled blue of his eyes.

"There are things we need to talk about."

"Not now. Let's pretend the real world doesn't exist."

"But it does exist." And in the real world, what he'd done would cost him his best friend, at the very least. And there might be an even higher price to pay, he thought, flattening his hand over her stomach.

"No future, no past." Colleen caught his hand and brought it to her face, pressing her cheek into his palm. "Until the snow melts, it's just here and now. You and I. The rest of the world doesn't exist. Please."

No one knew better than he that it was impossible to isolate yourself the way she wanted. The past was always there and the future couldn't be set aside forever. But he couldn't stand firm against the plea in her voice, against the need in her eyes.

"No future. No past," he agreed huskily.

Her smile was warm enough to melt the cool voice of reason that tried to tell him what a mistake he was making.

Chapter 7

When Gun woke, he was aware of several things at once. The first was that the cabin was chilly. The second was that the sun had gone down while he slept, leaving the interior of the cabin dark as a tomb. He noted both the temperature and the lack of light absently. The main focus of his attention was on the woman draped across his chest, making a very intriguing blanket. And on the heels of that realization came another, which was that he was already more than half-aroused.

Colleen.

It was Colleen who sprawled so invitingly across him, her soft curves pressed intimately against the hard angles of his body, her hair tumbling over his shoulder. With every breath he took, Gun could smell the warm, musky scent of their lovemaking, mingling with the sharp, clean smell of soap and the ever-present woodsy scent of the fire.

He stared into the darkness, waiting for the waves of guilt to crash over him. When they didn't come, he searched deeper. He'd just made love to *Colleen*, his best friend's sister. He felt a distant ache at the thought of the friendship he'd just forfeited, but he couldn't find the regret he knew he should be feeling.

He slid his hand up the length of her spine, savoring the smoothness of her warm skin. He knew what he should feel, but he kept remembering how right it had seemed, as if it had been destined.

Yeah, right, Larsen. Destiny didn't have a damn thing to do with it. You just made love to a girl you've known all your life, a girl you had no business touching—a virgin no less.

But the harsh voice of his conscience seemed muffled and unimportant. And the thought of Colleen's virginity didn't inspire the guilt he knew he should feel. Instead, he felt a wave of purely masculine possessiveness, a savage satisfaction that he'd been the first, that his was the only body to know the velvet tightness of her, to feel those sweet contractions as she came apart in his arms.

Major politically incorrect, Larsen.

Yeah, but it didn't change the way he felt.

Colleen shifted and Gun bit back a groan as her thigh brushed across his hardening flesh. It would be so easy to roll her onto the bed, to slide between her legs and wake her to trembling passion. But remembering the tightness of her body, the faint resistance he'd felt as she adjusted to his presence within her, Gun knew that while it might ease his own ache, making love to her so soon after the first time would be nothing short of abusive.

With a sigh of regret, he shifted her weight from him and slid off the bed. The covers were a wild tangle, but he managed to tug one loose and drape it over Colleen, though it seemed almost a crime to cover such beauty.

He pulled on his jeans, which he found by tripping over them. He tugged the zipper up but left them unsnapped, more concerned with getting a lamp lit and feeding the fire, which had obviously nearly died while he was busy tending another, more elemental fire.

Ten minutes, five matches, two singed fingers, a stubbed toe and several muttered curses later, Gun had a lamp lit and was carefully feeding the nearly dead fire in the little stove, coaxing the coals back to sullen life.

That was how Colleen saw him when she opened her eyes. Crouched in front of the stove, the flickering flames casting red-tinged shadows onto his bare chest, his hair falling in thick golden waves across his forehead. There was something wild and pagan about the image. If she narrowed her eyes a little, it was possible to imagine that the faded jeans were actually a breechclout, that the stove was a fire pit and the solid log walls of the cabin actually tanned buffalo hides.

As if sensing her gaze, he turned his head. Their eyes met and, despite her desire to appear cool and sophisticated, Colleen felt her skin heat. She unconsciously tugged the blanket a little higher.

"Hi." As a sophisticated morning-after kind of greeting, it could have been worse.

"Hi."

She was relieved Gun looked away, returning his attention to the fire. He shoved two small logs into the stove and shut the door before standing. Colleen was suddenly struck, in a way she never had been before, by just how large he was. Or maybe it was just that she was suddenly feeling rather small and vulnerable.

"I was just thinking that you'd look very good in a breechclout," she said, not wanting to let the silence stretch, even for a moment.

"Not many blond, blue-eyed Indians," Gun commented.

"Not unless you believe those legends about that lost Irish tribe. Or was it Welsh? They were supposed to have sailed to this continent in canoes. Or maybe it was the Polynesians who did that?" She knew she was rattling on like an idiot, but she couldn't seem to shut up. "Maybe this bunch came in some other kind of boat. Made out of hides or something. Anyway, they were supposed to have settled in Florida. Or was it Arizona?"

Gun started toward her and she talked even faster, hardly aware of what she was saying. "No one's ever proved there was such a group, of course, but I took a course in folk history once and the professor said there's often a kernel of truth in—"

The spate of nervous chatter ended on a squeak as Gun's hands closed over her upper arms and dragged her upright, blanket and all. Colleen caught a quick glimpse of oddly tender laughter in his eyes before his mouth closed over hers, stopping her words and sending her pulse rocketing.

He took his time with the kiss, and by the time he lifted his head, Colleen's arms were wound around his neck and her skin was flushed with a heat that had nothing to do with the fire he'd just built.

"Thank you." She dragged her eyes open and looked up at him. "In a few minutes, I'd have started reciting the Declaration of Independence."

"English lit courses?" He threaded his fingers through her hair, brushing it back from her face.

"American history," she corrected. She leaned into him, letting him support her weight. "I guess I'm not sure what proper behavior is for the morning after."

"Actually, it's the middle-of-the-night after and I don't know if Miss Manners has specific etiquette, but I doubt if a history lesson is on the recommended list of topics."

Colleen flushed, but the gentle teasing in his voice took any possible sting from the words. She lifted her chin and pursed her lips.

"I've always thought one should take education wherever one finds it," she said pedantically. "Learning should be an ongoing process, not confined to the class—"

Having found it effective before, Gun silenced her with a kiss. This time, when he lifted his head, Colleen could only cling to him, sure that she'd collapse like an overcooked noodle if he were to release her.

"Did anyone ever tell you that you talk too much?" he asked as he nibbled her ear, sending shivers racing up her spine.

"You did. You always used to complain that I talked more than any six people and Kel—" She broke off as she felt him stiffen at the mention of her brother's name.

He pulled away, steadying her as she sank back onto the bed. Colleen automatically pulled the blanket up to her throat, though the chill she felt was not the sort it could ward off. She couldn't believe she'd been so stupid as to mention Kel. Ridiculous as it was, Gun seemed to feel that, in becoming her lover, he was betraying his friendship with Kel. It was stupid, but it was one of those male things and there was no arguing with it. But she had to try.

"This . . . what's happened between us . . . has nothing to do with Kel." She gestured with one hand, encompassing the cabin and the bed they'd shared.

"I don't think he's going to see it that way," Gun said in a flat voice.

"It's none of his business."

"I doubt he'd agree."

"Maybe I don't care what he agrees with," she snapped, exasperated by his stubborn insistence that Kel had a right to approve or disapprove of her actions. "I'm a grown woman and I don't have to ask his approval for anything I choose to do."

Gun shook his head, plainly unconvinced. "We'll deal with it later."

"There's nothing to deal with!"

"I was right. You do talk too much." He dragged her up off the bed again, kissed her soundly and then released her. Colleen collapsed bonelessly amid the tangled covers. "But I don't mind shutting you up."

It was a unique, effective and not-unpleasant method for closing a subject, she decided as he walked away. Not that it was permanently closed. Sooner or later, they were going to have to deal with this idea he had that Kel had anything to do with what was happening between the two of them.

"Are you hungry?" Gun asked.

Colleen was surprised to realize that she was. It seemed such a mundane thing after all that had happened. "I could eat," she admitted.

"Stay there." Gun gestured her back when she moved to leave the bed. "I may not have gone to cooking school but I open a mean can."

While Gun was busy opening a canned ham and slicing it to go between biscuits leftover from lunch, Colleen snagged his shirt up from the floor next to the bed, flushing a little at the memory of how she'd nearly ripped it from him. She pulled it on and was rolling back the sleeves when Gun carried the plate of sandwiches over to the bed.

"What about crumbs in the sheets?" she asked as she reached for a biscuit.

"Eat carefully." He sat down on the foot of the bed, setting the plate between them.

They didn't talk while they ate, which suited Colleen just fine. She was having a difficult time believing that the past few hours hadn't been part of a dream. But there was a new awareness of her own body, a sort of tingling, alive kind of feeling paradoxically combined with an odd lassitude that told her it definitely hadn't been a dream. At least, not of the sleeping sort.

With the meal finished, Gun put away the food while Colleen straightened the bed. She was fluffing the pillows, which were so old that most of the feathers had migrated their way through the cover years ago, when she felt Gun's hands close over her hips.

"One thing about not having electricity—there isn't much to do after dark."

Colleen straightened, clutching the pillow she held to her chest. She could feel the warmth of his touch through the flannel and she was suddenly conscious of the fact that she was naked beneath the shirt.

"I...guess not." She had to swallow to get the words out. All he had to do was slide his hands beneath the tails of the shirt and he'd be touching her bare skin.

"There's no television, no VCR, not even a radio to listen to." As if reading her thoughts, Gun's hands found their way under the shirt.

"We could...read." She could feel the roughness of calluses against the soft skin of her hips.

"We could, but I've read just about everything there is to read." He nuzzled the back of her ear, sending shivers down her spine.

"I . . . haven't."

"Besides, we don't want to waste fuel. No telling how long we'll be snowed in." His teeth worried at her earlobe and Colleen felt a liquid heat start to pool low in her stomach.

"Could be a long time," she murmured breathlessly.

"I guess we'll just have to find something else to do."

"Do you have any ideas?"

"One or two," he murmured against the side of her throat. "One or two."

His hands drew her back until she felt denim against her bare bottom, felt, too, the hard length of his erection. He pressed against her for a moment and then turned her in his arms, his hands sliding up her back, pulling the shirt up until it was bunched under her arms. Colleen was too busy burying her fingers in his hair and dragging his mouth to hers to notice the discomfort. By the time the kiss ended, she was panting and breathless, her body throbbing with arousal.

Her hands dropped to the waist of his jeans, her fingers trembling with need as she searched for the tab of his zipper. She looked up in surprise when his fingers closed over hers, stilling her hands.

His brilliant blue eyes glittered down at her. His face looked as if it had been carved from granite, the skin stretched tight over the cheekbones, his mouth pulled into a hard line.

"What's wrong?"

"I forgot." He seemed to be grinding the words out, as if they were painful. "It's too soon."

"It doesn't feel like it's too soon." She shifted her fingers under his, flattening her palm against the bulge beneath his zipper, half-shocked by her own boldness.

Gun sucked a breath between his clenched teeth and caught her hand, dragging it up to rest against his chest. "I mean it's too soon for you. I don't want to hurt you."

Considering the intimacies she'd shared with him—and certainly hoped she was going to share again—it was ridiculous to feel embarrassed, but she felt the color rise in her cheeks. This kind of intimacy was going to take some getting used to.

"You won't hurt me," she said.

"Are you sure?" He looked unconvinced.

"I'll tell you what." She wiggled her hand loose from his and lowered it to his waist again. "Why don't we take it one step at a time and I'll scream at the first sign of pain." The rasp of a zipper punctuated her words and Gun's eyes darkened as her hand found him.

He was already rock hard and aching, and the feel of fingers stroking his hot skin made it difficult to think. How was it possible for him to want her this much so soon after the first time? If he hadn't known better, he would have thought it had been months instead of a few short hours.

"Colleen . . ."

"Did anyone ever tell you that you talk too much?" She slid her other hand into his hair, drawing his mouth down to hers.

Gun gave up the argument.

They lay together in the narrow bed, her slender body curved around the harder planes and angles of his. Colleen stroked her fingers through the sweat-dampened hair on Gun's chest, savoring the intimacy of being able to touch him. She felt pleasantly sated, deliciously exhausted. She'd always known Gun would be a superb lover. Not that she had anything to compare him with, but she didn't need to, not when her whole body was replete with satisfaction.

"Why now?" His voice was a rumble beneath her ear. "Why me?"

Her fingers stilled momentarily and then continued their soft petting motion. She didn't pretend not to know what he was talking about, but she chose her words carefully, unwilling to lie but knowing that the full truth would do more harm than good.

"It felt right," she said slowly.

"It felt right?" Though she couldn't see his face, she knew his eyebrows had gone up, questioning her explanation. "You stayed a virgin until now and then slept with me because it felt right?"

And because I love you.

But he wasn't ready to hear that. She wasn't sure just how she'd be able to tell if he was ready but she knew it wasn't now.

"You know me, I'm a creature of impulse," she said lightly.

Gun frowned into the darkness, wishing he could see her face. He didn't particularly like her explanation as to why she'd chosen him as her first lover. "It just felt right" and "I'm a creature of impulse" didn't set well with him. Not that he could think of a reason that would have.

She must have sensed something of what he was thinking.

"Does it matter?"

He supposed there was no reason why it should matter. They were lovers and he couldn't lie to himself and pretend to have any real regrets on that score. He'd already admitted to a visceral satisfaction at having been her first—and only—lover. Further than that, maybe he'd be better off not thinking.

"It doesn't matter," he said finally. It came to him, even as he said it, that he was lying, but he shoved the thought away. No past, no future, they'd decided. And to that he could add, no thinking. Under the circumstances, it could only cause trouble.

The days that followed were magical. No past, no future was what they'd agreed to. That left only the present and that was more than enough.

"That's the dumbest-looking snowman I've ever seen." Gun tilted his head and examined their joint creation critically.

"He is not!"

Colleen flashed him an indignant look before turning her attention to the somewhat lopsided snowman they'd spent the morning building. With chunks of half-burned wood for his eyes, a stick for his nose, a row of small rocks for his mouth and a juice can perched at a jaunty angle on top for a hat, he might not exactly be a thing of beauty but she liked him. She reached out to smooth one lumpy shoulder with her gloved hand.

"Besides, you shouldn't say things like that where he might hear you."

"He doesn't have ears," he said pointedly.

"Of course he does. They're just hidden. Like...like a wombat's."

She met his surprised look with an expression of such openness that Gun immediately became suspicious.

"You don't even know what a wombat looks like, let alone where its ears are."

"I do, too. I studied natural history for two whole semesters. They're from Australia," she said firmly, pulling out the one fact she was sure of.

"What are they?"

"What are they?" She stalled for time.

"That's right. What are they?" He put his hands on his hips and waited, eyes narrowed on her face.

"They're a sort of Australian bat, of course." She managed to sound scornful that he'd have to ask. "The 'wom' part of their name comes from their mating call, which is a sort of...*wom wom* noise."

From the look on his face, she suspected she'd stretched a bit too far with that last bit.

"You are lying through your pretty white teeth."

"My orthodontist thanks you."

"You don't have the slightest idea what a wombat is, let alone what their mating call is."

"That *could* be it," she protested, backing away as he advanced.

"*Wom wom?*" he repeated. "You expect me to believe that there are Australian bats that fly around going *wom wom?*"

"I don't see why not."

"Because I'm not as dumb as...as that snowman."

"Could have fooled me."

His eyes narrowed threateningly, the only warning he gave before lunging toward her. With a shriek, she dodged and ran away, though the deep snow made it more a case of floundering away.

Gun could have caught her anytime he chose and they both knew it, but the fun was in drawing out the game, running and dodging, laughing like a pair of children. It ended in the only way it could have, with Gun tumbling Colleen into a snowbank and holding her there while he demanded a retraction of her insult. Pouting, she said it wasn't fair to punish her for the truth. He tickled her ruthlessly for her obstinacy.

Lying together as they were, it wasn't long before Gun's hands found more interesting territory and laughter gave way to softer sounds. She offered no objection when he picked her up and carried her into the cabin.

"You never did tell me what you're doing up here." Colleen lay cuddled against Gun's side, her leg snuggled with casual intimacy between his, the fingers of one hand threading idly through the dark gold hair on his chest.

"Pretty much the same thing you came up here for," Gun said. "I wanted time to think and this seemed like a good place to do it. Kel gave me an open invitation years ago and I took him up on it."

There was a subtle hesitation when he mentioned Kel, but Colleen chose not to pursue it. Time would show him how foolish he'd been to worry about Kel's reaction to their changed relationship. Why he thought Kel would object to his best friend and his sister getting involved was beyond her.

"I came up here to figure out what I want to do with my life," she said. "What were you thinking about?"

"Pretty much the same thing, I guess." He brushed his hand idly up and down her back. "I thought it was time to make some decisions about the future."

"What kind of decisions?" She longed to ask if those decisions might have changed since her arrival, but she didn't quite have the courage for that. Not yet.

"Whether or not to settle down, I guess. I've been kicking around the country since I was a kid. I was wondering if it was time to light someplace and sit a spell."

There was a wistfulness in his words that tugged at Colleen's heart. She'd never given much thought to Gun's wandering ways. Ever since she could remember, Gun had been in and out of her life. He'd show up and work on the Lazy B for a few months and then he'd be gone. It had been three years since she'd seen him this time but there had been other gaps—a year, eighteen months. Gun had always wandered in and out of her life and she'd never thought to question the reasons. She knew he worked for other ranchers besides Kel.

"What about your father?"

Though her words were quiet, Gun tensed as if they'd carried a bite. "What about him?"

"Why aren't you working on his ranch? Why don't you ever go home?"

In the silence that followed her question, Colleen had time to review what little she knew about Gun's father. Ben Larsen had the ranch that neighbored the Lazy B. She'd seen him in town a few times, a large, red-faced man with a perpetual scowl.

She knew Gun had left home when he was sixteen and she'd heard someone say that Ben had threatened to shoot his son if he ever set foot on the place again, but no one seemed to have any real idea as to what the split between father and son might be about.

She knew that Gun's mother had died when he was a boy and that Ben had remarried, but she wasn't sure whether that had come before or after Gun left home. She'd seen the second Mrs. Larsen only once as she drove through town in a sleek car as ill suited to the rough Wyoming roads as the woman had looked to being a ranch wife.

"It's a long story," Gun said when she'd nearly given up hope of him answering her question.

"I don't have any appointments to keep." She tilted her head back until she could see his face. His smile was fleeting.

"The details are pretty boring." The lightness in his tone was forced and failed to reach his eyes. "My father and I never did get along and things didn't get better after my mother died."

"How old were you?"

"Fourteen."

"That must have been very hard for you."

"It was." The flat agreement told her just how hard it must have been. She rubbed her cheek against his shoulder, offering wordless comfort. "My father remarried less than a year later. I didn't take it well."

"I wasn't sure if he'd remarried before or after you left."

"It was before."

"That must have been very hard, seeing someone else in your mother's place."

"Vanessa wasn't the motherly type," he said dryly. "It wasn't her I resented so much as the fact that he'd married so soon after my mother's death. I don't know why it bothered me. He was a piss poor husband when she was alive. I shouldn't have been surprised when he didn't spend any time grieving."

"Of course it bothered you. You were just a child."

"I was old enough." There was an old bitterness in his voice, and when she lifted her head to look at him she saw him staring at something she couldn't see, his eyes steel blue and brooding.

"Did you quarrel with him?" She was more than half-sorry she'd brought the subject up, but she felt compelled to hear the rest of it.

"We quarrelled."

Colleen waited but he didn't add anything to those flat words. "And you left?" she prompted.

"I left. He threw me out." He shifted restlessly against the sheets. "I'm not sure which it was."

"Didn't you ever go back? Try and talk to him? Make things right?"

"There are some things that can't be made right."

Silence fell between them. Colleen tried to imagine what it must have been like for him. No matter what he said, he hadn't been more than a boy, and to find himself on his own, without family, seemed incomprehensible to her. Her own mother had abandoned her and Kel when Colleen was just a baby so she wasn't much inclined to idealize families, but she'd always had her father and Kel; she'd never been completely alone.

"It's funny," Gun said suddenly. "I was glad to go, glad to get away from him. And in all these years I've never missed the old bastard. But the ranch is something else entirely. I didn't realize how deep my roots went or how much it's possible to miss a place."

There was an emptiness in the words that made Colleen ache for the loss he still felt. She'd have given anything to be able to soothe his pain, but there were no words she could offer.

Gun felt her stillness against his side, heard the echo of his own words and was shocked to realize he'd said as much as he had. He hadn't talked to anyone about his father in over twenty years. He'd left home with a suitcase, a black eye courtesy of his father's fist, fifty dollars in his pocket and a self-hatred that had taken years to dissipate, if it ever really had.

He'd walked the ten miles to the Bryan place because he had nowhere else to go, arriving after midnight. Not wanting to wake anyone, he'd sat on the front porch to wait until morning. He'd fallen asleep somewhere in the dark hours before dawn and hadn't awakened until Kel's father had all but tripped over him.

Patrick Bryan had taken him in the house, put a cup of coffee in his hand, put a bandage on the small cut below his eye and accepted Gun's statement that his father had thrown him out with no more than a nod of the head. Despite the friendship between their sons, there'd never been any love lost between Ben Larsen and Patrick Bryan.

Kel's father had offered Gun a job, given him a place to stay and never questioned the reason for the final blowup. Not even Kel knew the whole story of what had happened between him and his father.

"It must be hard, not being able to go home." At the sound of Colleen's quiet voice, Gun shook himself free of the web of memories.

"I don't think about it much," he said and heard the emptiness inside call him a liar.

Chapter 8

Though neither Gun nor Colleen mentioned it, it was impossible to ignore the fact that the weather was warming, the unexpected cold snap grudgingly giving way to the push of spring. A week after they became lovers, it was obvious that the snow was thinning in places where the sun reached it. And the icicles that sparkled along the eaves of the little cabin were melting, dripping icy cold water on the head of anyone foolish enough to linger on the front stoop.

Unspoken between them was the feeling of time running out. There was an added urgency to their lovemaking, a certain sweet intensity to each day that passed. And hovering over everything was the question of what was going to happen when they had to leave the cabin and rejoin the real world.

* * *

Gun woke suddenly, his heart beating too quickly. Dream images danced just out of reach, fading before he could grab hold of them, leaving him with nothing more concrete than a vague feeling of something precious lost forever.

Colleen slept beside him, her back to his chest, his knees drawn up under hers. He lay still, listening to the steady sound of her breathing, letting his heartbeat slow to normal. Outside the cabin, he could hear the soft sighing of the wind. A chinook, melting the already-thinning snow, ushering in spring.

Gun's mouth tightened. He'd never taken less pleasure in the signs that winter was ending. There was no real excuse for staying in the cabin, he admitted grudgingly. Even carrying double, Satan could now make it down the mountain without undue strain.

He'd stayed longer than he'd intended already, and if it hadn't been for Colleen he would have left days ago. As long as he was being completely honest, he might as well admit that he'd have left more than a week ago, before the day they'd become lovers. He'd lingered because of Colleen, because he wanted to spend time with her, even when every scrap of common sense was telling him to get out while he could.

Well, he hadn't and they'd become lovers. And he'd undoubtedly lost a good friend in the bargain, he thought grimly. Colleen could insist all she liked that what she did was none of Kel's business, but Gun didn't think Kel was going to agree. When Kel found out that his best friend and his little sister had gotten considerably more than friendly, he was going to want Gun's head on a platter.

The only way Kel wouldn't find out was if he and Colleen went back to being "just good friends." And that just wasn't possible. The days when he'd been able to treat Colleen as his best friend's little sister were over, never to return. He waited for a feeling of regret that didn't come. It was difficult to regret the change when the woman lying against him felt so completely right in his arms.

Even if he'd wanted to conceal their changed relationship from Kel, there might be a reason that that would prove impossible. His hand had been resting on Colleen's hip. He shifted it now, spreading his fingers against her flat belly as if he could tell by touch whether or not a new life grew there.

After that first time, there'd been no mention of birth control. Madness, he'd whispered at the time even as he'd given in to the sweet temptation of her body. But temporary insanity couldn't explain the past week when he'd made love to her time and again, giving no thought to the risks they were taking.

It came to him suddenly, with a stark honesty only possible in the dark hours of the night, that he wanted to see her carrying his child, wanted to see her grow ripe and round, to know she cradled his baby within her body.

He'd lived for so long without home or family, telling himself he didn't need either. But he'd been wrong. There might be men who could drift through the world, never sinking roots in any one place, but he wasn't one of them. He wanted a home. And he wanted a son or daughter to hold, a reason to build a future.

His hand shifted subtly on Colleen's stomach. As if in response to that touch, she stirred, turning onto her back. Moving carefully, so as not to wake her, Gun propped himself on one elbow and looked down at her. The light of a full moon spilled in through the open curtains and brushed pale fingers across her face, catching in the thickness of her lashes, dusting the short straight length of her nose and dancing lightly over the fullness of her mouth.

Gun felt desire stir thick and warm in his veins. They'd made love only hours before, falling asleep in each other's arms. But it seemed as if he could never have enough of her, never slake the hunger that burned in him every time they touched.

Without considering his actions, he skimmed the softest of kisses across her mouth, returning again and again, as if drinking sweet nectar from a luscious flower. Colleen stirred, sighing gently as her mouth shaped to his in a sleepy kiss that made his pulse race.

Gun lifted his head when it ended, watching as her lashes slowly lifted.

"Gun."

Her voice was husky with sleep, but there was a languorous hunger in the way she stretched against him, her fingers threading through the curling hair on his chest.

"You could be carrying my child right now," he said, staring down at her with shadowed eyes.

Colleen stilled as she felt his hand against her stomach. She sensed something in him she didn't recognize. They hadn't talked about that possibility since the first time they'd made love and they hadn't exactly had a real discussion about it then. Her brain still sluggish with sleep, she couldn't even begin to analyze what was the right thing to say.

"I've always wanted a child."

"My child?" There was an urgency in the question, a need she couldn't help but respond to. She gave him the stark truth, uncaring of what it might reveal.

"More than anything," she whispered, her hand covering his where it lay on her belly.

"Colleen." Her name was a breath against her skin as he bent to kiss her. There was passion in the kiss but there was something more, a need, a hunger that seemed as deep as his soul. Colleen responded with every bit of love she felt for him, communicating by touch the feelings she didn't dare say out loud.

By the time he lifted his head, her eyes shimmered with tears. She blinked them aside, staring up at Gun, cursing the moonlight that shadowed his face, concealing his expression.

"I want you." His words seemed both plea and demand. His eyes glittered down at her, unreadable in the darkness.

"Yes."

She could feel his arousal pressed against her hip, could feel her own hunger rising to meet the need that burned in him.

There was an urgency in his touch she'd never felt before, an urgency that translated itself to her so that she twisted in his arms, tugging at his shoulders, her legs opening for him as she urged him to complete their union. Gun eased his fingers through the soft triangle of curls that guarded her femininity, seeking proof of her readiness, groaning when he found it.

Unable to wait another minute, he rose above her, his hands easing her legs wider as he settled into the cradle of her thighs. Colleen's breath caught as he tested himself against her, entering at first only a tiny bit, then withdrawing, only to return, deeper this time but not deep enough to ease the ache inside her.

"Please, Gun." The words were a plea, but the bite of her nails on his hips made them a demand.

Gun's mouth stretched in a purely masculine smile as he gave her what she wanted, sheathing himself in the hot depths of her, hearing her whimper echo his own groan of satisfaction at the feel of her around him.

But the satisfaction was only momentary. He wanted more. With her, he always wanted more. It was a hunger of the soul. A hunger he could only satisfy, albeit temporarily, in the yielding warmth of her body.

Colleen whimpered again as he withdrew almost completely, teasing her with the possibility of losing him. Her fingers dug into the muscled strength of his hips as she lifted herself, trying to force him to fill her emptiness. He hesitated a heartbeat longer, waiting until she was almost mad with the strength of her need and then he thrust into her again.

He repeated the pattern, the sensual threat to end their lovemaking, then the momentary slaking of her hunger, until Colleen thought she'd go out of her mind. The tension building inside her was almost painful in its intensity.

If he didn't stop, she'd shatter into a thousand pieces.

And if he did stop, she'd surely die.

Just when she thought she couldn't stand another minute of his sweet torture, Gun seemed to reach the limits of his own endurance. His hands slid beneath her bottom, tilting her hips up. Instinctively Colleen lifted her legs, locking her ankles against the small of his back. She cried out at the depth of his penetration, the tension in her trembling on the edge of explosion.

At the sound of her cry, Gun froze, locked deep inside her, his body going taut. "Did I hurt you?"

"No. Don't stop now. Please, Gun. Please." Her hands were damp on his shoulders as she arched beneath him, shaking with desire.

The blatant need in her voice was nearly enough to trigger his climax, even without the delicate contractions he could feel gripping him where he lay inside her. With a sound that was close to a growl, he eased nearly out of her and then thrust into her. Once. Twice. And she came apart in his arms.

His jaw clenched with effort, he rode out her completion, rocking against her to prolong her pleasure, feeling sweat break out along the length of his spine with the effort of holding back his own hunger.

Colleen drew a breath that was half a sob as she started the slow, delicious tumble from the heights he'd taken her to. But Gun had other ideas, and before she had time to catch her breath he was moving within her, fast and hard, driving her headlong into another climax, this one so powerful that she thought her heart would surely stop. And then she knew it had as he thrust one last time, penetrating deeper than ever before, seeming to touch her very soul.

With a guttural groan that was torn from deep inside, Gun gave in to the shuddering pulse of completion, feeling the complementary contractions of Colleen's most feminine heart as she took his seed into her body.

And he knew, with a knowledge he didn't think to question, that in that instant, they'd just created a child.

It was long, trembling minutes before Gun could gather the strength to move. Colleen murmured a protest as he eased his body from hers. Supporting his weight on his elbows, he leaned down to kiss her, tasting the depth of her satisfaction in the soft warmth of her mouth.

Lifting his head, he stared down at her, his hand shifting to lie flat against her stomach. Her much-smaller hand covered his, her moonlight-shadowed eyes looking up at him. They stayed that way for the space of several slow heartbeats, sharing the knowledge of the miracle they'd created.

Without speaking, Gun eased his arm beneath her shoulders, drawing her close as he sank onto the pillows. She curled into his body, snuggling her face into his shoulder. He felt Colleen relax against him, heard the soft rhythm of her breathing as she fell asleep as quickly and easily as a child.

The moonlight blurred before his eyes as a deep, visceral tiredness washed over him. He had only a moment to wonder at the feeling of peace stealing through him before he fell asleep. The kind of deep soul-healing sleep he hadn't known in a very long time.

A warm wind rushed softly around the corners of the cabin, melting the last traces of ice from the eaves. Moonlight spilled through the window, shifting patterns of light and dark across the couple sleeping in the narrow bed, so closely entwined that not even a shadow could slip between them.

Chapter 9

In the clear light of morning, the night just passed took on an almost dreamlike quality. Gun stood in the doorway and watched the water dripping from the eaves and considered the possibility that he'd been hallucinating. Maybe it was just something about waking in the middle of the night like that, some fantasy created out of the night shadows.

The idea that he could actually have known the moment that Colleen conceived a child was absurd. That kind of thing only happened in books. In real life, you waited six weeks and then consulted a little plastic stick to see if it turned pink or blue.

Even more incredible was the fierce exultation he'd felt in that moment of knowledge. Only a deranged man would actually have *welcomed* the idea of a pregnancy under the circumstance. Of course, the fact that they'd been risking just that for the past week or so called his sanity into serious question, but he wasn't quite ready for the men in the white coats.

Looking at the sunshine glittering against the retreating snow, Gun reminded himself of all the reasons why Colleen getting pregnant would be an unmitigated disaster. Thanks to their pact to live only in the present, they hadn't discussed the future—their future—at all. He didn't know what she wanted to happen when they left here. Hell, he didn't know what *he* wanted.

No, that wasn't quite true. He knew he didn't want it to end. He knew he wanted to see what might be between them outside the artificial world the storm had created for them. She'd brought to life feelings he hadn't known he was capable of. He wanted a chance to figure out just what those feelings were.

"The snow's melting," Colleen said from directly behind him.

"Yeah." Gun stared out at the sunshine a moment longer and then turned to look at her. "We can leave anytime."

Her teeth worried her lower lip as she nodded. "I know. We're running low on food."

"Sooner or later Kel is going to find out you're not where he thinks you are and then he'll start tearing the country apart trying to find you."

"I know." She sighed as she lifted her eyes to his face. "I knew we couldn't stay here forever," she said.

The wistfulness in her voice made Gun's tone rougher than he'd intended. "Nothing lasts forever."

She tilted her head, her eyes holding secrets. "Some things do" was all she said.

Gun wished he felt half as sure of that as she sounded. He brought his hand up, sliding his fingers into her deep red hair, savoring the silken feel of it against his hand.

"We can leave tomorrow," he said gently.

"All right." Her eyes were too bright, but that was the only sign she gave of being upset about leaving the cabin. Still, Gun felt the need to defend the decision.

"I've been here longer than I'd planned and I doubt you were going to camp this long."

"No," she agreed. She glanced past him at the clearing around the cabin. "If it hadn't been for the storm, I'd probably have been home days ago."

If it hadn't been for the storm, we wouldn't be lovers.

The thought lay unspoken between them. Gun knew he should regret the storm that had brought her to him, that had brought about such a drastic change in their relationship. But the only regret he felt was that it hadn't lasted longer.

Maybe he was going to have to start considering the insanity angle, he thought as his hand slid through Colleen's hair to cup the back of her head, tilting her face up for his kiss. But insanity or no, he was starting to think they should just let the rest of the world go hang.

But it seemed the decision wasn't theirs to make. Barely an hour later, the quiet was shattered by the sound of a snowmobile engine. Gun watched from the doorway as the machine glided into the clearing. The rider cut the engine and the sudden cessation of sound was almost shocking. Gun stepped off the porch as the man swung his leg over the seat of the machine and stood. He reached up to pull the goggles from his eyes, dropping them on the seat.

"Lije," Gun said, offering his hand by way of greeting. Lije Blackhawk had worked for Kel for a couple of years. Gun knew him as well as anyone on the Lazy B, which wasn't saying much since Lije kept to himself, not always an easy thing to do when sharing a bunkhouse with a dozen or more cowboys.

"Gun." Lije stripped off his glove and took Gun's offered hand. "Kel sent me to see if you were still up here."

"Problem?"

Before Lije could answer, his dark eyes cut past Gun's shoulder. Gun saw a flicker of surprise, gone so quickly it could have been his imagination. The quick crunch of Colleen's boots against the snow made him turn to see her hurrying toward them.

"Lije! Is something wrong at home?" She'd obviously heard Lije say that Kel had sent him.

"Miss Bryan." Lije nodded politely. "Everything's fine at the Lazy B."

"Oh, good." Tension drained out of her. Her fingers curled around Gun's upper arm. Lije took in the casual intimacy of the gesture without so much as a flicker of reaction. "Kel isn't looking for me, is he?"

"Not that I know of," Lije said. "I was looking for Gun."

"You found me." Gun wished Colleen had stayed in the cabin. The last thing he wanted was for Kel to find out about him and Colleen from a third party. Then again, Lije was about the least likely gossip he could think of. He'd met fence posts that were more talkative.

"Kel wanted me to give you this." Lije pulled a folded piece of paper from his jacket pocket and handed it to Gun. "Said I should stay and see if you needed help with anything."

Help with anything? Gun's brows rose. Why would he need help? A quick scan of the note gave him his answer. Kel's scrawl was brief and to the point. Gun's father had died of a heart attack. The funeral was in two days and the lawyer had said Gun's father wanted him there for the reading of the will. Kel hadn't added any condolences, knowing better than anyone that they'd be wasted.

"What is it?" Colleen asked, her eyes searching.

"My father died," he said without expression.

"Oh, Gun!" She pressed her face to his arm in a quick gesture of sympathy. "I'm sorry."

"Yeah." He started to say, "Me, too," but stopped when he realized how false the words would sound. He didn't know whether he was sorry or not. His ties to his father had never been particularly strong, even before he left home. Certainly he didn't feel any particular grief at the news.

"I need to get back," he said, narrowing his eyes against the glare of the sun off the snow. "Can you take Colleen back with you?"

Lije nodded. "No problem."

Colleen offered no protest. It was the most practical arrangement. They'd been planning to leave tomorrow, anyway. "I'll get my things," she said and turned back toward the cabin.

Gun started to follow her but hesitated, turning to look at Lije. "I'd appreciate it if you didn't say anything to Kel about finding Colleen here with me."

"None of my business." Lije said, lifting his shoulders in a half shrug.

Gun nodded and turned to follow Colleen into the cabin. She had already put on her coat and was pulling her knit cap over her hair. She reached for her gloves as he entered the cabin.

"There's a lot we need to talk about," he said without preamble.

"I know." Her smile shook around the edges. "You know where to find me."

"Yeah." He watched her tug on her gloves. "I don't know why my father would have wanted me to hear the reading of the will. Unless he just wanted the pleasure of knowing I'd be there to hear him leave everything to Vanessa."

"Maybe he didn't leave it to her. Maybe he was sorry for what had happened between you." She came over to him and put her hand on his chest, looking up at him with clear green eyes. "Maybe he wanted to apologize."

"You didn't know Ben Larsen." Gun's tone was dry but his smile was tender. He liked seeing the concern in her eyes.

"*You* hadn't seen him in a long time," she reminded him. "People can change."

"People can, but not my father."

Colleen shrugged and abandoned the argument. There were so many other things to talk about and so little time. Gun must have seen the frustration in her eyes.

"We'll talk," he assured her. "I'll come by the ranch."

"And face Kel?" she asked lightly, raising her eyebrows.

"It's got to be done." His tone was grimly rueful.

"You still think he's going to want to draw and quarter you, don't you?" She leaned her head against his chest, savoring the feel of his strong body, half-afraid it might be the last time.

"I think you're underestimating your brother's protective instincts."

"I guess we'll just have to wait and see which one of us is right."

"Yeah." Gun had other things on his mind besides Kel's temper. He cupped his hand over the back of Colleen's head, tilting her face up to his. "I don't know what my father had up his sleeve. If he came up with some legal nightmare to entangle me in, it could take a while to get away."

"I'm not going anywhere."

She sucked in a quick breath when he pressed his other hand over her stomach. "You'll call me."

She nodded, caught by the intensity of his eyes. "One way or another," she promised huskily.

There was so much more to say, Gun thought, searching her face. But Lije was waiting. Besides, he wasn't sure what he'd say, anyway. Colleen came up on her toes, meeting him halfway as his mouth covered hers. The kiss expressed frustration, hunger and the underlying fear that everything was changing so quickly.

The kiss ended. With a last look, Colleen turned and hurried outside as if afraid to linger. Gun followed more slowly. Lije was standing next to the snowmobile, showing no sign of impatience at the delay.

Gun pushed his hands in his pockets, watching as Lije helped Colleen onto the snowmobile. Once she was settled, he turned back to Gun.

"I'll take care of her." It was his only acknowledgment of the obvious intimacy he'd witnessed between Gun and Colleen.

"Thanks."

Gun stayed where he was while Lije started the snowmobile and turned it back down the mountain. He saw Colleen look over her shoulder but couldn't read her expression. She lifted her hand in farewell and then his view of the machine was blocked by the trees.

His hands jammed in his pockets, Gun walked back to the cabin, trying to ignore the hollow feeling in his chest.

* * *

It had been twenty-four years since Gun had set foot in his father's house, but everything was just as he remembered. The hardwood floors were a little more worn than they had been, as was the heavy oak furniture his mother had bought shortly after she married his father.

The upholstery was faded and worn through in places, but it was the same black-and-white striped linen he remembered from his childhood. Ben Larsen had always groused that it made him feel as if he was in a prison, all those damned black-and-white stripes.

Vanessa had evinced little interest in putting her stamp on her new home, but Gun was mildly surprised his father hadn't changed the furniture once Addie died. If Gun had been the sentimental sort, he might have thought that the fact that nothing had changed after his mother's death was an indication that Ben had wanted to keep some trace of his first wife around. But it was more likely a case of indifference and tightfistedness.

That tightfistedness had extended into all facets of his life, marking Ben's friendships as well as his financial dealings with the result that most of the people who'd come to the house after the funeral were there to pay their respects rather than to share their grief. Ben Larsen had caused too much grief in life to inspire much of it in death.

Gun became aware of the silence rippling through the room as people noticed him standing in the entrance to the living room. His friendship with the

Bryan family had kept him in touch with most of the ranchers in the area, but no one had expected to see him here. At the funeral maybe, but not here at the house.

They all knew Ben had threatened to shoot his son on sight if he ever set foot on the property. With some men that might have been an idle threat, but there were more than a few who believed Ben meant every word. But Ben was gone now and Gun had come home for the first time in over two decades.

The momentary silence was broken by a woman's voice, low and husky.

"Gun."

The newly widowed Mrs. Larsen made her way through the scattered groups of people, moving with the boneless grace he remembered. Vanessa had been a model before she'd married his father and she still carried herself as if hearing the click of a shutter.

"I'm so glad you could make it." Gun took the hands she held out to him, feeling a sharp amusement when he saw what she was wearing. Her dress was the requisite black, but the finely draped wool crepe was so stylishly sophisticated that it made a mockery of the idea that she was in mourning.

He was aware of the speculative looks being cast in their direction and wondered if some of the guests were hoping that a few discreet or not-so-discreet fireworks might erupt between the new widow and the black-sheep son.

"Vanessa." He ignored the slight tug of her hands, the subtle uptilt of her face. He was only willing to carry the happy-family act so far and that stopped short of kissing his stepmother's cheek. If she was offended by his refusal to play the game to its full extent, she didn't let it show.

"It's been a long time." She let her eyes drift over him, starting with the ruffled gold of his hair, skimming over the dark blue Western-cut shirt and jacket he wore with a pair of crisp black jeans and ending with his worn but freshly polished black boots.

"I don't think I'll ever get used to the idea of wearing jeans to social occasions," she said, the words more comment than criticism.

"My white tie and tails were at the cleaners," he said, offering no apology for the way he'd dressed. He freed his hands from hers. "You look well, Vanessa."

"Well?" She drew her perfectly reddened mouth into a moue of distaste. "Is that the best you can manage after all these years, Gun?"

He took his time answering, letting his gaze wander over the perfect oval of her face. She'd been twenty-three when she married his father. At fifteen, he'd found it difficult to imagine any woman more exquisite. The years had been kind to her. Or more likely, Vanessa had been kind to herself, he thought cynically. At forty-eight, she was stunningly beautiful. Her sleek dark hair showed not a trace of gray and any small lines that age had painted in her face had been artfully camouflaged.

She looked, he thought dispassionately, damned good. And she knew it. Which was why he phrased his answer the way he did.

"The years have been good to you, Vanessa. You hardly look your age."

Fury flashed in the pale blue eyes that made such a striking contrast to her dark hair. Gun saw her fingers curl into her palms and wondered if she was going to go for his eyes. But the tension left her an instant later. Her smile was a little forced around the edges but it was still a smile.

"You've changed, Gun." The words were a compliment.

"I'm not a boy of fifteen anymore."

"No, you're most definitely not that." Her eyes slid over him again, appraising him in a blatantly feminine way. When her gaze met his again, she made no effort to conceal her approval of what she'd seen. Her tongue flicked over her lower lip, like a cat scenting a dish of cream. "You're *definitely* not a boy anymore."

Gun wondered if she found that particular approach effective with men. That there'd been men besides his father he didn't doubt. Vanessa wasn't the type to let details like marriage vows get in the way of what she wanted. He wasn't sure what he would have said or done if he hadn't happened to catch a glimpse of fiery auburn hair across the room.

Colleen.

"Excuse me, Vanessa." She was forgotten even as he uttered the polite apology. Gun brushed past her and made his way toward Colleen, unaware of Vanessa's speculative look as she turned to watch him.

The Bryan family, consisting of Kel, his wife, Megan, and Colleen, were standing together near one of the windows. It was the sun spilling through the open curtains and tangling in Colleen's hair that had caught Gun's attention. It had been three days since she'd left the cabin. That didn't sound like long but after spending nearly every waking moment together for so long, three days seemed like an eternity.

"Gun." Kel saw him first, smiling and holding out his hand.

Gun took it, feeling like a traitor as he shook it. "Kel. Megan." His smile came more naturally for Kel's wife. Even if he hadn't liked Megan for herself, he would have liked her for the joy she'd brought to his friend's life. "How's the holy terror?"

Megan smiled at his description of her son. "Michael's fine. I'm sure he'd be glad to see his Uncle Gun anytime you cared to visit."

"I'll do that soon," he promised, keeping his smile in place as he finally let his eyes settle on Colleen.

"Hello, Colleen." He wondered if he was the only one who noticed the flush in her cheeks. He took the hand she offered, feeling the jolt of that small contact go through him like electricity. If they'd been alone, he'd have pulled her into his arms and kissed her until they both had to come up for air.

"Hello, Gun."

Colleen felt her color deepen as she saw the blatant hunger in Gun's eyes. Though he'd only touched her hand, her skin felt suddenly sensitized so that even the soft linen of her dress felt almost unbearably harsh.

Gun released her hand slowly, letting his middle finger stroke across her palm. The light touch sent a shiver down her spine and nearly melted her knees.

"You're back from school, I take it," he said.

"Which school?" Kel's voice was dry. "There've been so many I've lost track."

"I'll graduate one of these days," Colleen told him, dragging her eyes from Gun.

"Before or after they put me in a nursing home?"

"I have to do something with the money Mother left us," Colleen said. "You won't touch any of it."

"Conscience money." There was old bitterness in the words. Megan reached out to take her husband's hand. Kel took it and seemed to make a conscious effort to lighten his voice. "I suppose she might as well have been good for something, even if it is financing your exploration of every educational institution in America."

"I don't know if I'll make it to all of them," Colleen protested.

"You've got a running start, Short Stuff."

She winced at the old nickname, not sure she wanted Gun reminded of her former pigtailed self. But Megan was already changing the subject.

"Do you have any idea why you were asked to be here for the reading of the will, Gun?"

He shook his head. "Dad's lawyer is tight-lipped enough to work for the CIA. All he'd say was that my father wanted Vanessa and me together when the will was read."

Before anyone could comment on this require-
ment, Vanessa's husky voice slid into the conversation, the same way her hand slid around Gun's elbow,
Colleen noticed.

"I'm sorry to interrupt, but there are some people
who'd like to speak with you, Gun."

Gun hesitated. He wanted to talk to Colleen, but he
couldn't do that in front of Kel. And he wanted to talk
to Kel, but this was hardly the time or the place.

"Go on," Kel said, taking the decision, if there'd
been one, out of his hands. "We'll catch you later."

"I'll be in touch." Gun's nod included the three of
them, but his eyes lingered longest on Colleen and she
knew the words were intended for her.

The gathering didn't last very long. It didn't take
much time to say the few good things that could be
said about Ben Larsen and it didn't seem fitting to say
the truth when the man wasn't even cold yet. Besides,
there was work to be done. Ranching didn't slow down
for death and there were chores waiting and a long
drive to face for most of the guests.

The Bryans were among the last to leave. They were
on their way to the door when Michael's kindergarten
teacher waylaid them. Colleen adored her nephew, but
she wasn't particularly interested in hearing about the
school bazaar to be held in a few weeks so she drifted
a few feet away.

Though she'd done her best to avoid it until now,
she couldn't resist letting her gaze linger on Gun. He
was talking to an elderly rancher, his blond head bent

as he listened attentively to whatever the man was saying. Colleen bit her lip as a wave of love and longing swept over her.

"Handsome, isn't he?"

Startled, Colleen's head jerked toward Vanessa, who'd suddenly appeared beside her.

"Handsome?" she repeated, trying to gather her scattered wits.

"Gun." Vanessa nodded her head in his direction, but her eyes never left Colleen's face. "He's handsome, don't you think?"

"Y-yes." Infuriated to hear herself stammering like a schoolgirl, Colleen drew a deep, calming breath. "I don't think you'd find anyone who'd argue with you."

"He was a beautiful young man," Vanessa said, letting her eyes drift to her stepson. "Like a painting of a Renaissance angel before the fall." Her eyes cut back to Colleen, making the other woman feel like a bug under a microscope. "I think angels are much more interesting after they've gotten their hands a little dirty, don't you?"

"I've never given it much thought," Colleen said truthfully.

Just what was the woman getting at? Was there a point to this conversation or was Vanessa simply rambling? Maybe she was so grief stricken that she didn't know what she as saying, though she looked more bored than grief stricken.

"I'm sorry about your husband's death, Mrs. Larsen." Colleen tried a more normal conversational branch. She realized suddenly that she was feeling more than a little intimidated by the older woman's beauty. Though she'd met Vanessa before, she didn't remember feeling quite so overshadowed by her.

"Are you?" Vanessa's expression was unreadable.

"Of course I am." She was only interested in Ben Larsen's death insofar as it affected Gun but she'd expressed the expected regrets as a matter of courtesy.

Vanessa's cool eyes watched her as she drew deeply on the cigarette she held between long, perfectly manicured fingers.

"No one liked my husband, Miss Bryan. And no one's sorry that he's dead. Including myself. If you'll excuse me, I see someone I want to speak to." And with that, the newly widowed Mrs. Larsen glided off, trailing the scent of expensive perfume.

Colleen stared after her, feeling as if she'd missed something. She had the feeling that Vanessa's words had been intended to put her in her place as much as for shock effect, but she wasn't sure why Vanessa would have felt the need to do either.

Kel and Megan had finished their conversation with Michael's teacher and were standing near the door, waiting for her so they could leave. Gun was across the room. Colleen let her eyes linger a moment on his tall figure. She'd hoped to be able to speak to Gun alone, but it was obvious that wasn't going to be possible.

Stifling a sigh, she went to join Kel and Megan. She'd just have to be patient a while longer.

Gun stepped into his father's den and felt painful old memories sweep over him. How many times

had he been called in here to be told of some new fail-
ing? He'd spent the most miserable moments of his
childhood in this room, listening to his father tell him
how utterly worthless he was. This was where they'd
had their final confrontation, the one that had ended
with Gun leaving home forever.

Or so he'd thought. But he was home again.
Twenty-four years older and, he hoped, wiser, but
home. For a moment, he almost expected to see his
father sitting behind the wide mahogany desk, his blue
eyes, so like Gun's own, hard with anger. But the man
who rose from the big leather chair had none of Ben
Larsen's size and none of the fierce bitterness that had
tightened the other man's mouth and chilled his eyes.

"Gun. Good to see you again."

"Myron." Gun reached across the desk to shake the
smaller man's hand, smiling in genuine pleasure. Myron Hickman came as close as anyone to calling Ben
Larsen a friend. He had a small outfit a few miles east
where he raised horses and a few head of cattle. He
was also a lawyer and one of a small handful of people Gun's father was willing to concede might be honest.

"Hope you don't mind me using Ben's desk," Myron said, gesturing to the battered briefcase and the
small stack of papers that occupied the dusty surface.

"I don't mind, but it's not me you should be asking. I assume it's Vanessa's desk now." It was as close
as Gun could come to asking why he was here, why his
father had wanted him present for the reading of the
will.

But Myron refused to be drawn. "Where is Mrs. Larsen? We can't start without her."

It struck Gun suddenly that, in a part of the country noted for its casual form of address, how few people he'd heard use Vanessa's first name. It was interesting that, after all these years in the community, she'd managed to remain a stranger.

"I'm here," Vanessa said before Gun could answer Myron's question. Both men turned toward the doorway. "I just wanted to freshen up a bit. I thought I should look my best to hear my dear, departed husband's last wishes."

"If you'll sit down, we'll get started," Myron said.

"That bad, is it?" Vanessa's tone was lightly derisive, but Gun noticed that her hands were not quite steady as she sank into one of the two chairs Myron had arranged across the desk from himself.

"I think I'll stand," Gun said, in answer to the lawyer's questioning look.

"Very brave of you," Vanessa said mockingly.

"Actually, Ben's will is fairly simple." Myron settled a pair of glasses on his nose and glanced through the papers, though Gun doubted his memory needed refreshing. After a moment, he peered over his glasses at the two of them. "Do you want me to read the legalese to you or do you want it in plain English?"

"Plain English," Vanessa said crisply, dropping her languid air.

"Good." He shifted the glasses up his nose, shuffled the papers a moment more and then set them on the desk, aligning them neatly along the edge. Clearly he was enjoying the drama of the moment and in no rush to end it.

Gun realized that his hand, where it lay on the back of the chair he'd refused, was clenched into a fist. Drawing a deep breath, he forced it to relax.

Fool. Don't let yourself hope. There's not a snowball's chance in hell of getting the ranch.

Just when it seemed as if the tension had stretched to the breaking point, Myron cleared his throat again and tapped his finger decisively against the papers.

"Ben left the ranch to the two of you. Thirty percent to his wife, Vanessa Elaine Larsen. Seventy percent to his son, Gunnar Benjamin Larsen. That makes you majority owner, Gun." He peered over his glasses in Gun's direction.

"Why?" The single hoarse word was all Gun could manage.

"Ben said blood was important. Said three generations of Larsens had worked this place and he wasn't going to be the one to break the chain. So he left you the lion's share of the ranch.

"Ordinarily that would put you pretty much in charge of things, let you do just about anything you pleased. But Ben added the proviso that you can't refuse Mrs. Larsen the right to maintain residency on the ranch, nor can you sell your portion of the ranch to anyone but her. And she can't sell to anyone but you."

The silence that fell after he quit speaking had much the same quality as the aftermath of an explosion. Gun stared at Myron, his mind reeling with the idea that the impossible had occurred.

The quiet was broken by Vanessa's harsh laugh. "The old bastard finally got his revenge." She laughed again in answer to Gun's blank look. "Don't you see? He's made us partners and arranged it so we'll be living together."

Gun ignored her, interested in only two things.

The ranch was his.

He'd come home to stay.

Chapter 10

One of the advantages of living in the country was the fact that your neighbors left their doors unlocked, Colleen decided as she used her foot to push open the back door of the Larsen ranch house and stepped into the kitchen. Unlocked doors eliminated the messy task of breaking and entering.

One of the disadvantages of living in the country was the fact that everybody knew everybody else, she thought as she carried her two sacks of groceries to the counter, sighing with relief as she set them down. Another trip to her car, to bring in a bottle of wine and a carefully arranged bouquet of flowers. They joined the groceries on the counter.

She surveyed her booty with satisfaction. The food, the wine and the flowers had all been purchased in a town nearly an hour's drive away. If she'd bought them locally, there'd have been a chance that some-one would mention to Kel that his little sister had been buying wine and flowers and then Kel would have asked her about it. She certainly didn't want to lie to him, but she could hardly tell him that she was plan-ning on seducing his best friend.

It had been two weeks since she'd seen Gun after his father's funeral. It seemed like about a thousand years. She understood why he hadn't come to see her. At least, she hoped she understood. Kel had told her about Ben Larsen's will. Remembering Gun's com-ment about how much he missed the ranch, she'd been thrilled to hear that he was finally able to come home again.

Kel had been to see Gun the day before, and at din-ner he'd told her and Megan what Gun was up against, inadvertently giving Colleen an explanation for Gun's absence. In the past few years, Ben had been letting things slide. Fences and equipment hadn't been re-paired; the stock had received only cursory care; in places, the cattle had been allowed to overgraze. It would take years to repair the damage done to the range in those areas.

Gun was going to have his hands full, Kel had said, shaking his head over the condition of the ranch. And with spring calving in full swing, it was going to be a while before he'd have time to draw a full breath. At least, it looked as though his stepmother wasn't going to cause problems. She'd left for New York the day after the funeral and hadn't been heard from since.

It was that piece of information that had resulted in Colleen's presence in Gun's kitchen now. If Vanessa was gone, Gun was alone in the house. And if Gun was alone in the house, there was nothing to stop her from paying him a visit.

It was the neighborly thing to do, she told herself. Though "neighborly" might not be exactly the right word for the black silk panties and bra hidden under her jeans and teal green cotton shirt. She'd been tempted to wear a dress, preferably one designed to make a man sit up and take notice, but that was another thing she didn't want to have to explain to her brother.

Colleen sighed as she began to unpack the makings for chicken cordon bleu. It was obvious that she wasn't cut out for a clandestine affair. She didn't like lying to Kel, even by omission. She wanted to tell him about her and Gun. Of course, at the moment, it was a little unclear just what she'd say.

Did she and Gun even have a relationship to tell her brother about?

Two weeks ago, she'd have answered with a resounding yes. When she'd left the cabin, she'd carried the heat of Gun's last kiss with her. She'd been confident that, while Gun might not be in love with her yet, they were at least on the right track. But after two weeks of silence on his part, doubts had begun to creep in.

Maybe Gun was regretting what had happened between them at the cabin. Maybe the reason he hadn't called wasn't because he'd been so busy but because he wanted to forget their time together. If that was the case, then she was about to completely humiliate herself. Her hands were not quite steady as she finished unloading the bags and folded them into very neat rectangles.

Nothing ventured, nothing gained.

The trite phrase hadn't sounded as hollow earlier as it did now. Colleen swallowed hard, struggling against the urge to stuff everything back in the bags and go back the way she'd come as fast as her car would take her.

Gun *did* care for her. She hadn't imagined the tenderness in the way he'd touched her, held her. In coming here, she wasn't trying to push him into anything, but she desperately needed some reassurance that she hadn't dreamed those days on the mountain.

She drew a deep breath and picked up the apron she'd brought with her. Shaking it out, she pulled the strap over her head and cinched the ties around her narrow waist. The way to a man's heart was supposed to be through his stomach, though she'd heard it suggested that the actual path started a bit lower. Either way, she was covered. If chicken cordon bleu didn't make him realize what he was missing, then maybe black silk underwear would.

Whichever, Gun was in for a surprise when he got home.

The last thing he needed was another surprise, Gun thought. He slammed the truck's hood down and pulled a rag from his pocket to wipe the grease from his hands. Not that it was a surprise to find that the truck needed carburetor work. After what he'd seen the past two weeks, the surprise was that it wasn't something more major, like a new engine.

Stuffing the rag back in his pocket, he put repairing the carburetor near the top of his mental list of jobs that needed to be done. The problem was, it seemed like just about everything on the list should go near the top. Everywhere he looked, there was something demanding immediate attention.

He turned away from the truck and headed toward the house. He walked slowly, his eyes going over the collection of buildings that centered around the main house. He still couldn't believe that the ranch was his. He couldn't remember that his father had ever shown any signs of family feeling before, certainly nothing strong enough to suggest that he'd leave the ranch to a son he hadn't seen in almost a quarter of a century, rather than let it go out of the family. Even in giving Vanessa a part of it, he'd made sure she couldn't sell it to an outsider.

Gun's frown deepened at the thought of his stepmother. She'd left right after the funeral and he hadn't heard from her since. It had been a relief. He had enough to deal with right now without adding Vanessa to the mix. Not that his father had left him any choice in the matter. His seventy percent of the ranch might put him in charge but Vanessa was still a part owner and she had the right to express her opinion about the way the ranch was run and to continue to live there.

The latter thought made him shudder. God knew, he had no desire to share a house with her, or anything else for that matter. If she was right and Ben had left the ranch divided the way he had out of some need for revenge, he just might have achieved his goal.

As if the condition of the ranch wasn't revenge enough. Gun thrust his fingers through his hair and considered the possibility that his father might have deliberately let things slide, knowing what a mess he'd be leaving for his son. There wasn't a thing on the place in decent shape—from the vehicles to the buildings to the stock.

According to the ranch foreman, Ben had started to let everything go a couple of years before.

"Seemed like he just didn't give a damn," Bill Granger had said a few days after the funeral. He and Gun had been looking at a mediocre herd of cattle and an overgrazed section of land. "I done what I could, but with the wages he was willing to pay we couldn't hire decent hands. Couldn't even hang on to the trash we did hire."

He leaned from his saddle and spit a stream of tobacco juice into the scrubby grass. "It weren't just the wages, neither. Bunkhouse roof leaks like a sieve and your daddy had a temper like a Brahma bull on a bad day. And her." He spit again, his expression disgusted. Gun didn't ask who Bill was talking about. He didn't have to. "She wasn't no more use than teats on a boar. A troublemaker from the start, that one. Had to fire more than one man 'cause of her."

Bill had been foreman when Gun was a boy and he didn't hesitate to speak his mind.

"Did my father know what condition the place was in?" He chose not to pursue the topic of Vanessa for the moment. Gun found it hard to imagine any rancher letting his land deteriorate this way.

"He'd of had to been blind not to," Bill said bluntly. "And I told him besides. Told him I'd seen sheep country in about the same shape."

"What did he say?" Gun knew his father had held with the old line that sheep ruined the range. Being compared to a sheep rancher would have been about the worst possible insult.

"He fired me."

"But you're still here."

Bill leaned over to spit another stream of tobacco, wiping his mouth with the red bandanna he kept tucked in his shirt pocket for the task. The look he slanted Gun held a touch of dry humor.

"I don't take to bein' fired."

Gun grinned. There weren't many men who'd been willing to stand up to his father's temper. He'd have given a lot to have seen the confrontation between the two men.

"I'm glad you stayed on."

"This is my home," Bill said simply. "I've been here most of thirty years and I'm too damned old to be pullin' up stakes and findin' myself a new job. Besides, if I'd of left, there's no telling what kind of shape this place would have got to."

Remembering the conversation a week later and having seen still more evidence of the ranch's neglect, Gun was doubly thankful for Bill's refusal to be fired. But not even Bill's devotion had been able to make up for his father's indifference. It was going to take years to repair the damage to the range and to rebuild the herd. In the meantime, there were miles of fences to be mended, the bunkhouse roof to repair, the house to be painted and every piece of machinery was either unusable or close to it.

When he let himself think about it, it seemed an overwhelming job. But the ranch was his—seventy percent, anyway. And he'd work himself into the ground to put it back into good shape, if for no other reason than to keep his father from winning.

Gun's boots thunked on the wooden steps of the back porch. He noted absently that the railing was cracked on one side and should be replaced. But that could wait. At the moment, he wanted a hot shower and dinner, which would consist, as it had for the past couple of weeks, of a plateful of sandwiches that he could carry into the den where he could sort through the stacks of paperwork that filled every drawer of his father's desk.

He pushed open the back door and stepped into the kitchen. And stopped dead.

Colleen was standing at the counter, neat piles of vegetables in front of her and a knife in her hand. The kitchen smelled of fresh-baked bread and other aromas he couldn't immediately identify.

Seeing her, it struck him that he couldn't imagine a more perfect end to the day than walking into the house and finding her there. It had nothing to do with the smell of bread or the pleasures of a hot meal. He could hire someone to provide those.

But he couldn't hire someone who'd make the tension ease from his shoulders just by being there. Seeing her, he felt an odd shifting inside, as if something was clicking into place.

The light greeting Colleen had planned to offer died unspoken. Gun was looking at her so oddly that she felt her stomach jump with quick tension. Did he think she'd overstepped the undefined boundaries of their relationship?

Gun took his hat off and hung it on one of the hooks beside the door. Still without speaking, he crossed the floor toward her, his boot heels clicking on the linoleum. He stopped in front of her. Colleen stared at his collar, afraid to lift her eyes to his face, afraid of what she might see. Had she made a huge mistake?

And then his hand was curving over the nape of her neck, his thumb tilting her face up to his. She caught just a glimpse of the sharp blue of his eyes before his mouth covered hers, assuring her that he was definitely *not* angry.

Gun took his time, exploring her mouth with a thoroughness that drained the strength from Colleen's knees. By the time he lifted his head, her fingers were wound into the fabric of his shirt, holding on for support. She let her head fall against his chest while she struggled to regain her breath.

Gun held her, one hand flat against her back, the other buried in her hair. Colleen was pleased to hear the rapid thud of his heart beneath her ear, proof that he'd been affected as much as she had. He smelled of sunshine and sweat and grease, an intensely masculine combination.

"I parked my car where you couldn't see it and broke into your house," she said when her breathing had steadied a little.

"I'll call the sheriff in a minute." He nuzzled her hair.

"I ransacked your kitchen."

"It probably needed it." His tongue found the sensitive skin behind her ear.

"I'm cooking you dinner." The words were breathless.

"Mmm." He seemed more interested in assuaging an entirely different kind of hunger.

"I wanted you to see what I could do with something that wasn't canned or dried."

He mumbled something against her ear just before his teeth closed over the lobe, biting gently and sending a shiver down her spine.

"It's chicken cordon bleu." She tilted her head back, offering him the arch of her neck.

"Good." It was difficult to tell whether his comment applied to the chicken or to the pulse that beat at the base of her throat.

"I made a chocolate cake." Colleen hardly knew what she was saying, but Gun was not quite so far gone.

"Chocolate cake?" His head came up. "*Real* chocolate cake?"

Colleen wondered if she should feel offended by his abrupt shift of interest.

"*Real* chocolate cake." Her lower lip thrust out in the merest suggestion of a pout. "With chocolate frosting."

"Well." Gun drew the word out, giving it a couple of extra syllables as he eased back from her. "I wouldn't want all your hard work to be for nothing."

"I appreciate your concern." There was a snap in her voice and her pout had become more definite.

"It's not every day a man has a chance for a home-cooked meal," he said solemnly. "And I sure wouldn't want to hurt your feelings."

The subtle exaggeration of his drawl brought Colleen's gaze to his face. While his expression remained as serious as his tone, his eyes gleamed with laughter. It struck Colleen suddenly that she must have sounded ridiculous, describing a meal while he nibbled on her ear. If she hadn't been so nervous about seeing him again...

"Some people would appreciate the trouble I went to," she said severely. Her cheeks flushed red, rivaling her hair, which she'd pulled back from her face with a pair of combs.

"I do appreciate it. I just appreciate you more."

Colleen allowed her ruffled feathers to be smoothed by his blatant flattery. Still, there was no sense in letting him off the hook too easily.

"I could always feed your portion to the dog."

"What dog?" Gun reached out to snitch a chunk of tomato, moving too quickly for the swat she aimed at him.

"I could drive into town and find one," she threatened darkly.

"A dog wouldn't appreciate you half as much as I do," he swore. Ignoring her halfhearted attempt to dodge him, Gun caught her around the waist and planted a solid kiss on her mouth. He released her as quickly as he'd grabbed her, grinning when she put a hand back to brace herself against the counter.

"I'll go clean up." Taking advantage of her momentary weakness, he snitched a handful of matchstick carrots and sauntered out of the kitchen.

Colleen watched him go. She'd never seen Gun in quite that mood. He'd seemed almost...boyish. Moving slowly, she turned back to the counter and picked up the big chef's knife she'd brought from home, a relic of the days when she'd thought she might become the next Alice Waters.

As she sliced mushrooms with quick, deft strokes, she heard the water come on upstairs. A sudden image of Gun standing naked under a spray of water made the knife slip and only quick reflexes kept her from losing the tip of one finger. Colleen drew a deep breath and forced the image to the back of her mind.

There'd be time for that later; at least, she hoped there would be. Otherwise she'd worn her only set of real silk underwear for nothing. They could eat a nice civilized meal together, talk about what was happening in each other's lives, begin the process of figuring out just what their relationship was, establish a base for the future.

And then she could jump his bones.

Chapter 11

The meal was delicious, a testament to the months Colleen had spent in culinary school. Everything turned out picture perfect, from the tomatoes in vinaigrette that served as both appetizer and salad, to the chicken breasts stuffed with ham and Swiss cheese and cooked to tender perfection. The sautéed matchstick vegetables were the perfect degree of doneness, the rolls were delicate but substantial enough to satisfy a man who'd spent the day doing hard physical labor. Colleen doubted she'd ever achieve such culinary perfection again.

And it might as well be sawdust for all the attention either of them paid to it. Certainly Gun ate heartily. He worked too hard *not* to eat. But his eyes kept drifting to the woman across the table, to the way the light caught the fiery highlights in her hair, to the ivory perfection of her skin.

She was telling him about something her nephew, Michael, had done. Gun listened with half an ear. He thought Kel's little boy was nearly as perfect as Michael's aunt did and, ordinarily, he'd have paid more attention to the story she was telling. But tonight Michael's pranks couldn't hold a candle to the deep green of Colleen's eyes or the warm coral of her mouth.

It seemed as if it had been ages since he'd held her, touched her, felt her skin against his. He ate mechanically, his mind filled with vivid memories of Colleen in his arms. Her skin was as soft as it looked, so pale that he had been able to watch the delicate flush of arousal creep upward from her chest to her throat and finally to her face.

He forced himself to look away from her, aware of the sudden painful constriction of his jeans. He'd never in his life wanted a woman the way he wanted Colleen. There was probably a message to be had there but the blood thrumming in his ears made it difficult to think.

"Are you ready for cake?"

Colleen's voice brought Gun's eyes back to her face and she felt her breath catch at the blatant hunger in them. Her fork dropped from her fingers, clanking noisily against her plate. Neither of them noticed.

"Will the cake hold?" There was a guttural quality to his question that made an ache start somewhere in the pit of her stomach.

"Yes." She was vaguely surprised to find that she could get even that one whispered word past the sudden tightness in her throat.

"Good. Because I won't."

He was reaching for her as he stood and she went into his arms eagerly, her own arms circling his neck as he lifted her against his chest, her mouth opening for the sweet plunder of his tongue.

Gun carried her upstairs, finding his way by instinct more than sight. By the time they reached his bedroom, Colleen had his shirt half-unbuttoned and was pressing soft, hungry kisses along his collarbone. He set her on her feet, groaning as her body slid the length of his.

With fingers made impatient by the depth of their need, they pulled and tugged at each other's clothing. When the buttons on Colleen's shirt proved frustratingly small and recalcitrant, Gun solved the problem by tugging the garment off over her head. His shirt followed a second later.

A heartbeat after that, his hands slid beneath her unfastened jeans, his palms cupping her bottom, lifting her against the hardened ridge of his erection. His groan was echoed by Colleen's sharply caught breath. He held her that way only a second and then she was pushing against his chest, demanding to be set down.

"We're overdressed," she said breathlessly.

Grinning at her impatience, Gun put her down. She immediately attacked the fastening of his jeans. The button yielded and she had her fingers on the zipper tab when Gun groaned again, this time with frustration.

"Ah, damn!" His hand closed over hers, preventing her from lowering the zipper. Colleen looked up at him, her eyes reflecting her frustration. "We can't, honey. I wasn't expecting you. I'm not prepared for this."

"You feel prepared," she whispered, twisting her hand free and cupping her fingers over his fly.

Gun gritted his teeth and grabbed her hand, pulling it away. "Condoms, honey. I don't have any here. And I assume you're not pregnant or you would have said something by now."

"I don't know yet," she admitted.

"We're not taking any more chances the way we did on the mountain," he said firmly. "We shouldn't have taken the ones we did."

"You're right," she said meekly.

They were silent for a moment, tension humming between them. Gun's face was drawn taut with frustration and desire. Colleen stared up at him for a moment and then she leaned forward, flicking her tongue deliberately over the flat copper disk of his nipple. He jerked as if she'd taken a whip to him.

"Don't," he said hoarsely. "Don't make it any harder."

"I don't think it could get any harder," she whispered wickedly, bringing her hand back to the front of his jeans and tracing her fingers along the hard length of him. Gun's laugh was more of a groan.

"You're going to kill me."

"Put your hand in my back pocket."

"There's no sense in torturing each other like this."

"Just put your hand in my back pocket," she insisted. She scraped her fingernails over the fabric of his jeans, feeling him jerk in response to the caress.

Colleen watched his face as he put his hand in her pocket and felt the crisp little packages there. The frustration disappeared, replaced by pleased surprise. He pulled the condoms out and weighed them on the flat of his palm as he grinned down at her.

"Three?" His brows rose, his grin taking on a wicked edge as Colleen flushed. "I'm flattered."

"It's always best to be prepared," she said primly.

"I don't think I've ever been more prepared in my life."

He traced his fingers over the swell of her breast, his thumb flicking over her nipple, and the brief interlude of conversation was over as the urgency rushed back, all the more forceful for having been held in check.

The remainder of their clothing was stripped away and there was a sigh of relief as they touched, skin to skin, at last. There'd be time for lingering over the preliminaries later, time for all the soft sighs and whispered touches, time for the sweet torment of drawing the moment out. But not this time. This time the hunger was too great, the urgency too powerful.

Colleen sighed as she felt the coolness of the sheets come up under her back and she reached for Gun, wanting only to feel the heat of him over her. Within her.

He used his teeth to tear open the little packet.

"Wait. Let me." Colleen reached for the condom, but he shook his head.

"Not this time, honey. If you touch me now, we're likely to end this before it gets started," he said bluntly. He rolled the condom on with quick efficiency. "Sort of like locking the barn door after the horse may already be out," he muttered under his breath.

Colleen's laugh was brief. At the moment, all she could think of was how long it had been and how much she needed him to fill the emptiness inside her, an emptiness as much of the heart as it was physical.

Their coming together was explosive. He filled her with one thrust, sheathing himself in the heated warmth of her body. Her whimper of satisfaction changed to a keening moan of pleasure as he withdrew and then filled her again. Her hips arched to take him deeper. Her hands traced a frantic pattern on the taut muscles of his back as they strained together.

Gun fought to hold on to his control, wanting the sweet torment to last forever. But it was too powerful to last very long. She cried out as her pleasure peaked. Gun found himself spun into the whirlpool of her climax, his body tightening and swelling within her. He caught her hips in his hands, thrusting hard and fast, drawing out her climax even as he reached his own.

He collapsed against her, barely managing to support his weight on his elbows to avoid crushing her. He could feel tremors running up his spine, like aftershocks following a powerful earthquake. Which wasn't a bad description of what had just happened. It had certainly felt as if the earth moved.

Colleen's hands shifted against his back as she nuzzled her face against his collarbone. Impossible as it seemed, Gun felt hunger stir in him again. It was as if the wanting would never end, as if he could never slake the thirst he felt for her.

He tilted her face up to his, staring down into the warm green of her eyes, reading the satisfaction there, seeing the need that lay beneath it. With a groan, he lowered his mouth to hers.

"I'm not sure three is going to be enough," he muttered against her lips and heard a ghost of a laugh before her mouth opened to him.

Three was enough—barely. By the time Colleen left, she had to hold on to the banister going down the stairs because her knees were distinctly wobbly. She felt drugged with happiness, physically sated and emotionally satisfied. Gun hadn't said he loved her, but it was only a matter of time. She might not have a great deal of experience in the bedroom, but she knew Gun. He couldn't have made love to her with such aching tenderness if he didn't care for her.

At the foot of the stairs, he pulled her into his arms, kissing her with so much hunger it didn't seem possible that they'd just spent the past few hours in his bed.

"I wish you could spend the night," he said.

"So do I. But Kel would worry. I told him I was going to visit Jane Sinclair." Jane was an old friend of

Colleen's. They'd known each other since first grade and had remained close.

"I don't like you lying to him. I'll come over Sunday and talk to him." His expression was bleak and Colleen knew he thought that he'd be putting an end to his friendship with her brother.

"Kel knows I'm a big girl." She smoothed her fingers over the lines on his forehead. "I think you're wrong about how he's going to react. Why would he object? You're his best friend."

"And you're his baby sister, no matter how old you are. Kel isn't going to like the idea of you sleeping with anyone. The fact that I'm his friend is going to make it worse, if anything."

Colleen shook her head but didn't argue. This had to be one of those male things that women didn't understand. She thought he was wrong about Kel, but knew he wasn't going to change his mind.

"I'll be over Sunday," he said again.

"Sunday's five whole days away. I'm not sure I can wait that long."

"I probably need at least that long to recover." Grinning, he dropped a kiss on her nose. "Don't forget, I'm not a kid anymore."

"You seem to have pretty good stamina for an old man." She snuggled closer, enjoying the feel of his muscled body against hers.

"Clean living." He gave her such an impossibly virtuous look that Colleen laughed.

Naturally Gun had to kiss her into silence and it was several minutes before she dragged herself out of his arms. They were both breathless and flushed.

"I've got to go." She seemed to be asking more than telling, as if she were hoping he'd tell her otherwise. Gun nodded reluctantly.

"Yes. I don't want Kel—"

He broke off as the front door opened and Vanessa walked in. Apparently they'd been so absorbed in each other that neither of them had heard her car. An automatic flip of her hand shut the door behind her. The quiet thud as it closed was followed by a thick silence.

Vanessa looked from Gun, standing at the foot of the stairs, barefoot, bare chested, his hair tousled from both the pillows and Colleen's fingers, his jeans zipped but unbuttoned, to Colleen, who stood halfway to the kitchen door. She was fully dressed, but her thick red hair tumbled around a face flushed from loving, her lips were a deep coral, swollen from Gun's kisses.

Vanessa's dark brows climbed slowly as she reached some quite accurate conclusions. Her gaze flicked back to Gun and he felt his gut knot when he saw the malice in her look.

"Vanessa..."

"You look a little rumpled," she said, ignoring the warning in his voice and addressing herself to Colleen.

"I, um, I..." Colleen self-consciously combed her fingers through her hair, trying to smooth the tangled curls into order.

"Oh, don't worry, my dear." Vanessa's delicate laugh held a sharp edge. "I won't tattle."

"I…" Colleen glanced at Gun, wondering how she should respond, but his attention was focused on Vanessa. "Thank you," she said finally, at a loss for another response.

"Don't thank me." Vanessa set down her overnight case and snapped open a small black clutch purse, pulling out a cigarette and a gold lighter. She took time to light a cigarette before continuing. "Considering how much we have in common, we really should stick together, don't you think?"

"Dammit, Vanessa…" Gun took a quick step forward as Vanessa lit her cigarette.

"Don't get so testy, darling. Colleen's a big girl. I'm sure she understands these things."

Vanessa's words made Colleen uneasy. There was something about the other woman that made her uncomfortable, a glittering look in her eyes that implied that Vanessa knew something Colleen didn't.

"What things?" Colleen asked, not entirely sure she wanted to know the answer.

"It's not important," Gun snapped. He moved as if to step between them, but Vanessa, for all her indolent appearance, could move quickly when she chose. She sidestepped around him and faced Colleen again.

"What's going on?" Colleen glanced from Gun to his stepmother.

"He's really very good, isn't he?" Vanessa purred.

Colleen stared at her. It was suddenly very hard to breathe. "What are you talking about?"

"Exactly what you think I am." When Colleen continued to stare at her, Vanessa waved her cigarette, trailing smoke through the air between them. "In bed. He's very good in bed, isn't he?"

The blunt words left no room to doubt her meaning. And Colleen desperately wanted room for doubt. She wanted a whole lot of room for doubt. She dragged her eyes from Vanessa's face, looking past her to where Gun stood, his face drawn into tight lines.

"Gun?" Her voice shook, begging him to say something, to tell her it was a lie, a filthy vicious lie. Gun met her look for only a moment, but it was long enough for her read the truth.

"Oh, God." It was as if she'd just been kicked in the chest. Her lungs struggled to draw a breath and there was a terrible ache where her heart should have been. Putting the back of her hand to her mouth, she backed away. "Oh, God."

"Colleen." Gun took a step toward her, his expression agonized.

His movement broke the spell that had been holding her. With a sob, she turned and fled, through the kitchen where she'd dreamed such silly dreams, out the back door and into the safety of her car. Her fingers were shaking so badly, it was all she could do to fit the key in the ignition. But she managed it and an instant later the engine roared to life. Gravel spun from beneath the tires as she slammed the car into gear.

Tears blurred the road before her, but they couldn't blur the image of Vanessa in Gun's arms. In Gun's bed. That image was burned into her soul.

Gun heard the back door slam behind Colleen and started forward. Vanessa caught his arm, her slender fingers surprisingly strong.

"Let her go. She won't listen to you now."

She was right. From the look on Colleen's face before she'd turned and run, she wouldn't want to hear anything he had to say right now. Besides, what could he say?

He pulled his arm away from Vanessa's grip, listening to the sound of Colleen's car fading away. She was gone.

"Maybe I should have called to let you know I was coming home," Vanessa said lightly. "If I'd known you were going to be entertaining one of the local cowgirls, I wouldn't have just—"

She broke off as Gun turned to look at her, his eyes full of a contempt so fierce it bordered on hatred. For a moment, she looked almost frightened, but she quickly recovered her balance, though her soft laugh held a shaken edge.

"I think you're actually in love with your little cowgirl."

For the first time in his life, Gun briefly considered the possibility of punching a woman. He shook his head. It wasn't worth the effort. Besides, no matter what her motives, Vanessa hadn't told Colleen a lie. He was as much to blame for Colleen's hurt as Vanessa—more so, in fact. His anger was directed at himself as much as at his stepmother.

Without a word to Vanessa, he turned and walked upstairs, feeling years older than he had when he'd walked down them a few minutes before. Going into his bedroom, he shut the door and then stood there, staring at the love-rumpled bed.

I think you're actually in love with your little cowgirl.

Vanessa's mocking words rang in his head. Ironic that she should be the one to recognize what he felt. Even more ironic that he should only realize his feelings for Colleen now when it was too late.

Closing his eyes, he let the pain roll over him.

Chapter 12

Three weeks after her disastrous visit to Gun's house, Colleen bought a home pregnancy test kit and sat watching as the little plastic stick turned pink, confirming what she'd already known.

She was pregnant.

Sitting on the closed lid of the toilet, she stared at the little stick, her head spinning with conflicting emotions. Her first reaction was sheer, unadulterated joy. She'd known the chance she was taking when she'd made love with Gun in the cabin. She'd told Gun she would welcome having his child and she'd meant it. She still meant it. The thought of having a baby— Gun's baby... She couldn't even encompass the wonder of it.

Hard on the heels of her pleasure came pain. Nothing was the way it should have been. She should be sharing this moment with the baby's father, not sitting here alone, trembling on the edge of panic. Gun should be here to put his arms around her, to share the excitement of finding out that they were going to be parents.

Gun.

Even thinking his name hurt. She wanted to hate him. She did hate what he'd done. After what they'd shared at the cabin, how could he have slept with Vanessa? There had been no promises made but she hadn't thought she was the only one who felt the specialness of what they experienced. But obviously, she'd been wrong.

She wanted to hate him for the dreams he'd shattered but she still loved him. He'd been a part of all her dreams for so long. The feelings of betrayal roiling inside her weren't enough to smother those dreams completely. But dreams or no, she had to deal with reality. And the reality was, she was pregnant with Gun's baby.

Her mind spun with questions. How would he react? Was she even going to tell him about it? Where were she and the baby going to live? What about a job? What about a name for the baby?

Grimacing, she stood. There was plenty of time to worry about names and jobs and living arrangements. Plenty of time to worry about everything, including what, if anything, she wanted to tell Gun. She tossed the plastic stick in the trash and turned to look at her reflection in the mirror. It would be weeks be-

fore she began to show. Weeks before she had to make
any major decisions.

She smoothed one hand absently over her flat
stomach. She wanted to tell her brother. There were
enough secrets between her and Kel, she didn't want
another one.

As for Gun... Shaking her head, Colleen shoved
that problem to the back of her mind. She didn't know
what she wanted to do about Gun.

She decided to tell her brother and sister-in-law the
news that evening, waiting until they'd put Michael to
bed for the night and then saying that she had something important she wanted to tell both of them. They
were sitting in the living room, the television turned to
a news program. Kel was sprawled on the sofa, leaving little room for Megan. From the way she snuggled
against him, it was apparent that she didn't mind him
crowding her.

Colleen chose an overstuffed chair at a right angle
to the sofa and tried to look relaxed, which wasn't easy
when every nerve in her body was humming with tension.

"Don't tell me," Kel ordered, his tone teasing. "Let
me guess. You've decided on a new school. What are
you going to study this time? Botany? The sex life of
tree frogs?"

"Actually, I had something a little more basic in
mind." Colleen linked her hands together in her lap to
conceal the tremor in her fingers.

"Basic?" Kel's dark brows rose. "Nursing was basic. Cooking was basic. What's more basic than that?"

"Kel." Megan had noticed the trembling in Colleen's fingers, the general air of tension that hovered over her. She put her hand over her husband's knee and squeezed. "Let her get a word in edgewise."

"Thank you." Colleen drew a deep breath, held it for a moment and then let it out without speaking. She'd spent the whole day planning what to say, but now that the moment was here her mind was a complete blank.

Seeing her uncertainty, Kel frowned and sat forward on the sofa, reaching for her hand. "Is something wrong?" The gentle question immediately brought foolish tears to her eyes. She blinked them away and forced a shaky smile.

"Nothing's wrong. At least, *I* don't think it's wrong. But you might not agree. I hope you will but you might not."

Kel stared at her for a moment as he sorted through what she'd said. He cut right to the heart of it. "What do you think I'm going to be upset about?"

Colleen's teeth worried her lower lip as she struggled to find the right words. But in the end, she could only blurt it out.

"I'm pregnant."

Kel stared at her, his expression so blank that she wondered if he'd understood her. Then she saw the shock come up in his eyes and his fingers tightened over hers for a moment before he released her and sank back against the sofa, still staring at her.

"Pregnant?" It was Megan who asked the question, her soft features concerned. "Are you sure?"

"Yes. I used one of those home kits this morning. I was already pretty sure."

"And you're happy about it?"

"Yes." That was one thing she was absolutely sure of. No matter what the circumstances, she was very happy about this baby.

Kel heard the conversation as if from a great distance. He couldn't drag his eyes from Colleen, his Colleen—his little sister. He still thought of her as being just a kid. Despite the fact that she'd lived away from home off and on for the past six years, she was still hardly more than a child.

Yet she was sitting there, telling him she was going to have a baby. She wasn't old enough to have a baby! She wasn't old enough to—

"Who's the father?" The abrupt question made both women jump. "Are you getting married?"

"Kel." Megan put her hand on his arm, feeling the tightness of the muscles bunched under his shirt. "There's no reason to bark."

"I'm not barking," he barked. He stopped and sucked in a deep breath. When he spoke again, it was in a dangerously calm tone. "I don't think it's unreasonable to want to know who knocked up my little sister." He ignored Megan's sharp protest at the crude term. "And whether or not he plans on taking responsibility and marrying her."

"This is the 1990s, Kel. Not the 1890s," Colleen said, feeling her temper rise to meet his. "A woman doesn't have to get married just because she's having a baby."

"So he won't marry you," Kel accused. He shot to his feet, his big body tense with anger. "He'll change his mind once I get my hands on him!" He stalked over to the television and snapped it off with such force it was a wonder the knob didn't come off in his hand. "I'll wring his damned neck for him and then drag him to the altar!"

Colleen stared at him and then exchanged a helpless look with Megan. She hadn't expected this reaction at all. Kel had always been the very best of older brothers. Who would have thought that he'd react like a character in a Victorian novel?

"If you wring his neck, it won't do much good to drag his body to the altar," she said with a nervous laugh. Not that she saw anything particularly humorous in the scene. But it was either laugh or scream, and if she started screaming she wasn't sure she'd be able to stop.

"What's his name?" Kel, understandably, ignored her feeble attempt at humor.

"He's someone I know," she said evasively. She'd given it some thought and had already decided that she had no intention of telling Kel who the baby's father was. Certainly not before she'd decided whether or not to tell Gun.

"I assumed that," Kel snapped, pinning her with sharp green eyes. "*Who* is it?"

"I don't want you wringing anyone's neck or dragging anyone to an altar."

"I can't believe you'd protect the bastard after he got you pregnant and refused to marry you."

"He didn't refuse to marry me. He doesn't even know about the baby."

There was a moment's silence. When Kel spoke, his voice was very quiet, very controlled.

"You *are* going to tell him, though." The words were more statement than question.

"I don't know yet," she admitted. "I don't know."

Silence again and Colleen was aware of Megan sitting very, very still, her slim body tense, her eyes riveted on her husband.

"Don't you think he has a right to know he's going to be a father?" Kel asked quietly.

Colleen swallowed hard and took her time about answering. It was only now that it occurred to her how this situation might look to Kel. Megan had once disappeared from his life, taking his unborn child with him. She'd realized that she'd been unfair and had contacted him to tell him that he had a son. But Kel had lost the first two years of Michael's life. Now it looked as if her own situation might open up old wounds. She chose her words carefully.

"I only just found out for sure this morning, Kel. I need time to think this out for myself before I decide what to do about ... other things."

"We're talking about a man's right to know he's a father, Colleen. That doesn't fall into the category of 'other things.' Did he ... hurt you?"

"No! He'd never hurt me." She didn't want Kel to get that idea in his head. Sooner or later, he was going to find out who the baby's father was and the last thing she wanted was for him to think Gun had abused her in any way. He might have broken her heart but she knew that wasn't what Kel meant.

"Do you think he'd be an unfit father?" The question came with relentless calm.

"No." She knew, on some instinctive level beyond question, that Gun would be a very good father.

"Then why wouldn't you tell him?"

"I didn't say I *wasn't* going to tell him," she protested. He made her feel like a witness on the stand— a guilty witness. Trying to lessen the feeling, she stood and faced him. "I don't know what I'm going to do. But I'm hoping you'll support me, no matter what I decide."

Brother and sister stared at each other across the room, but it felt as if a gaping canyon had opened between them. There was conflict in Kel's eyes and a muscle worked in his jaw. Colleen looked at him with a mixture of pleading and determination. Neither wanted to give an inch.

"Kel." Megan broke the stalemate by going to her husband. Her small hand trembled when she set it on his sleeve. "It's Colleen's decision," she said softly.

Her breath caught when his eyes slashed to her face and she saw the old pain in them, muddying the clear green she loved so much.

"Even if she's wrong?" he asked harshly.

"Yes." She swallowed hard, knowing she was treading on very delicate ground. "You have to let her decide what to do and trust that it's the right choice."

Hanging in the air between them was the choice Megan had once made and the time he'd lost with his son because of that choice, time he could never regain. After a long moment, he dragged his eyes from hers and looked at his sister.

"I'll support whatever you decide." The words didn't come easily, but Colleen knew he meant them.

"Thank you." She managed a tremulous smile.

Kel cleared his throat. He looked down at Megan, his expression shadowed. "I want to check on that new horse we got yesterday. See if he's settling in."

Megan's teeth worried at her lower lip as she stared after him. Her expression lightened a little when he paused beside Colleen and drew her into a brief hug. Colleen watched her brother leave and then turned back to her sister-in-law.

"I'm sorry. I didn't stop to think that this might bring up old memories."

"Don't apologize. It's not your fault that I made the choices I did." Megan dragged her gaze from the doorway through which Kel had disappeared and forced a smile. "We worked it out a long time ago, but he can't help but remember. I can't give him the memories of Michael's first two years. I'm not trying to tell you what to do, but be sure you think about it carefully before you decide not to tell the father about the baby."

"I will."

"I'm really very happy for you, Colleen. And Kel will be, too, once he gets used to the idea that you're grown up enough to have a baby." Colleen returned her hug, grateful for the support. "I need to go talk to Kel." Though Megan smiled, Colleen could see the worry in her eyes.

She drifted upstairs after Megan left, thinking about the other woman's words. Think carefully, she'd said. That was one thing she could certainly promise.

Megan found Kel in the barn, leaning against the stall door, talking to the horse that had been delivered the day before, a stallion he hoped to breed with some of his mares. The big Appaloosa was watching Kel warily, seemingly intrigued by the man's quiet voice but wary enough to keep his distance.

"He's beautiful." Megan put her hand on Kel's shoulder, feeling the tension that knotted his muscles.

"Yeah."

"Colleen will be all right."

"It's a hell of a shock," he said, keeping his gaze on the horse.

"That she's pregnant? Or that she's older than twelve?"

His mouth quirked in brief acknowledgment of her teasing tone. "Both. She still seems so young to me."

Megan drew a deep breath. "I was only a little older when I had Michael."

The words hung between them. They rarely spoke of those two years when they'd been apart. It was as if, by ignoring them, they could somehow pretend they'd never happened. But they had happened and the hurt they'd caused wasn't going to disappear just because they wanted it to.

"Look at the choice you made," Kel said, after the silence had gathered too long. "Do you think you were right to keep Michael from me?"

"No." She stepped close, setting her hands on his chest, forcing him to look at her or move away. "I was wrong, but I thought I was doing the right thing at the time and no one could have told me any different."

"Just like I can't tell Colleen any different?" He looked down at her, his eyes unreadable in the shadowy barn.

"It's her choice. Trust her to make the right one."

"Do *I* have a choice?" At the touch of humor in his voice, Megan felt something inside her begin to relax. She shook her head, her eyes filling with foolish tears as his arms came around her, pulling her against his chest. They stood that way for a long time, the barn quiet around them.

"I can't help but think of all I missed." Kel spoke over her head, his voice low. "I never held him when he was a baby. I didn't hear his first word or see his first step."

Megan felt her heart twist at the pain in his voice, pain she'd caused him. Her hands slid up his shirt until her palms cupped his cheeks, feeling the roughness of a day's growth of beard. She tilted her head back, making no attempt to brush aside the tears that escaped.

"I can't give you back those years, Kel."

"I know." He bent to kiss the tears from her face, sorry he'd said anything. The last thing he ever wanted to do was cause her pain. "It's all right."

"If we had another child, I wouldn't let you miss even a second of his life."

"You don't have to have another baby just because I missed some of Michael's childhood." They'd talked about having another child, but Megan had wanted to wait until Michael was a little older, not wanting to make him an older brother when he was hardly more than a baby himself.

"Michael starts school this fall." Her fingers slid into the thick darkness of his hair and her body softened subtly against his. "I think this next winter would be a good time to give him a little brother or sister."

"You do, huh?" Kel's breath caught as she rocked against him, making the blood heat in his veins.

"I do." She rose on tiptoe to place biting little kisses along the length of his jaw.

"This winter. We'd have to get started pretty soon to manage that." He was surprised his voice was as steady as it was, considering the shock waves she was setting off.

Her hands linked behind his neck, she leaned back to look up into his face. Not so coincidentally, the movement pressed her hips solidly against his. Kel stifled a groan. "No time like the present," she suggested.

As he picked her up and carried her to the back of the barn where the hay was loosely stacked, Kel could only agree.

* * *

"You are *not* going riding." Kel set his jaw.

"I am, too." Colleen set her jaw every bit as firm as his.

"No, you're not. Not in your condition."

"Pregnant women ride all the time."

"Did a doctor tell you that?"

"You know I haven't seen a doctor."

"Then don't tell me what pregnant women do all the time."

It was an unanswerable point and she knew it. Perhaps she could give an inch or two.

"I won't gallop her."

"No, you won't," Kel said agreeably, "because you're not going riding."

Colleen barely restrained the childish urge to stomp her foot. "You are the most irritating, arrogant, pigheaded, annoying...male I have ever met in my life."

"I can say the same for you but substitute 'female.'"

They stood toe to toe in the middle of the ranch yard, eyes locked and glaring at each other. It wasn't that Colleen was so dead set on riding. But she was dead set on not letting him push her around. If he'd made it a suggestion instead of an order, she might have given in. But he'd *told* her what to do and her back had gone up and, before she knew it, they were arguing.

It was a scene they'd played, with variations, several times in the week since she'd told him about her pregnancy. She knew Kel's anger had more to do with the fact that she still hadn't told him who the baby's father was and that she still hadn't come to a decision about telling the father, whoever he was, about the baby.

She didn't like being at odds with her brother, but she had no intention of being rushed into any decisions. Nor was she going to tell him that it was his best friend whom he seemed to both want to strangle for getting her pregnant and yet couldn't help but defend his right to know he was going to be a father. God knew what would happen between him and Gun when Kel found out the truth.

The sound of a car coming up the road from the highway interrupted the glaring match. Colleen and Kel both turned to look at the visitor and Colleen thought she might faint when she recognized Gun's car. There weren't many fire-engine red 1967 Corvettes floating around.

"It's Gun," Kel said, his voice reflecting his relief at having a distraction. He glanced at Colleen but found that he'd spoken to himself. His sister had turned and was halfway back to the house. At least she wasn't going riding.

Gun stepped out of the car just as Colleen's back disappeared into the house. His eyes were bleak as he looked after her. How long would it be until she was willing to talk to him? Should he force the issue or just give her time? And how the hell could he force the issue without Kel finding out what had happened, which would probably result in him finding himself cas-

trated and shot before he had a chance to say hello to
Colleen again.

"Gun." Kel's welcome made Gun feel lower than a
snake's belly.

"Kel. Was that Colleen?" He knew it was but some
demon prompted him to ask. He shut the car door and
walked over to Kel.

"Yeah." Kel's mouth tightened and the look he
threw over his shoulder seemed to hold both anger and
concern.

"Problem?" *You're pushing your luck, Larsen.*

"You could say that."

Gun waited, knowing Kel would expand on his
comment if he chose, not sure he wanted to hear
whatever Kel might have to say. Kel hesitated a moment and then he lifted one shoulder in a shrug.

"It's not public knowledge yet but it will be sooner
or later."

"There's nothing wrong with Colleen, is there?"

If Kel hadn't been so wrapped in his own grim
mood, he might have noticed an unusual urgency in
the question. As it was, he shook his head.

"Not wrong, I guess." Kel's expression was bleak.
"She's pregnant."

"She's..." Gun couldn't get the word out. He felt
as if Kel had just slammed a fist into his solar plexus,
driving the air out of him. Colleen was pregnant.
"How long?"

He couldn't articulate the question any better than
that, but Kel seemed to know what he was asking.

"She told us about a week ago. I guess she's about six weeks along. I haven't asked for details."

Gun didn't hear anything past the first sentence. He knew far better than Kel could just how far along she was. His mind flashed to that last night in the cabin, the night when he'd had that odd, almost mystical flash of knowledge. The night they'd created a baby.

He focused his attention on the one piece of information he didn't have. A week. She'd known for at least a week and she hadn't contacted him. Did she hate him so much that she couldn't even bear to tell him that he was going to be a father? Did she think she could keep this information from him forever?

"If I get my hands on the sonofabitch who— Where are you going?" Kel broke off, startled as Gun walked past him.

"I have to talk to her."

"It won't do any good." Kel caught his arm. "You know what she's like, stubborn as a mule."

"You don't understand." Gun shook Kel's hand from his arm as he turned to look at him, his eyes glittering with emotion. "It's my baby."

Chapter 13

Colleen stared at the glass of milk in front of her, trying to conjure up some enthusiasm for drinking it. It wasn't that she didn't like milk. It was just that, since finding out about the baby, Megan had been pouring it down her every chance she got. It seemed as if glasses of milk appeared out of thin air and sat in front of her until they were consumed. Arguing did her no good. Megan simply pointed out that it was good for the baby and topped off her glass.

"I'm going to start mooing soon," she muttered.

"That doesn't happen until the eighth month or so." Megan was peeling carrots for supper and she glanced over her shoulder at Colleen's gloomy expression. "By then it won't matter anymore because you'll be so fat you'll feel like a cow, anyway," she said with ruthless good humor.

"Thanks. I feel a lot better now." Colleen picked up the glass and sipped the cold liquid absently. What was Gun doing on the Lazy B? Had he come to see her? To her disgust, the thought made her heart flutter. She didn't care if he'd come to see her. She didn't want to see him! Her unruly heart continued to flutter, oblivious to the dictates of her head.

The front door opened with a bang and the sound of small boots rattled across the hardwood floors. An instant later, her nephew burst into the kitchen.

"Mama!"

"Michael Kelly Bryan, how many times have I told you not to run in the house when you're wearing those boots." Megan's tone was exasperated.

"Sorry." Michael was too full of news to take time with his apology. "Mama, Daddy and Uncle Gun are out by the corral and they're rolling in the dirt and hitting each other and I heard Dick sayin' it looked like they was going to kill each other."

"What on earth?" Megan exclaimed, shocked.

Colleen was already on her way out of the kitchen, quick strides taking her into the den. Megan sent Michael upstairs, sternly denying his plea to watch Daddy and Uncle Gun kill each other. She saw him reluctantly head upstairs and then followed her sister-in-law.

"Colleen? What's going on? Good Lord, what are you doing with that?"

Colleen had a rifle in her hands, taken from the locked gun case in Kel's den.

"I'm going to save them the trouble of killing each other," she said grimly. She stood on her toes and pulled a book down from the shelf, flipping it open to reveal the shells hidden inside, well out of reach of small, curious fingers.

"What's going on?" Megan asked, feeling like Alice having just fallen down the rabbit hole.

"Men." Colleen said the word with revulsion, apparently thinking that explanation was all that was necessary.

"Well, yes. They can be rather annoying." Megan watched uneasily as Colleen slammed shells into the chamber. "I'm not sure shooting them is the answer, however."

"I am."

With that flat assurance, Colleen stalked past her and out the front door, which Michael had left open in his hurry to share the excitement with his mother. Megan followed her, telling herself that Colleen wasn't *really* planning on killing anybody. Was she?

It seemed as if most of the men were clustered near the corrals, watching their boss and his best friend do their best to inflict serious damage on each other. When Colleen shoved her way between Bob Mason and Carey Wills, the two of them were on their feet, hammering at each other. From the condition of their clothes, it was obvious that Michael's description of them rolling in the dirt hadn't been an exaggeration.

Looking at the two men she loved most in all the world, Colleen felt anger rise up in her. Her hands tightened on the stock of the rifle as she considered the possibility of bashing them both over the head with it. Instead, she pointed the rifle in the air and fired it. Before the echo of the first shot had died, a second followed it.

"What the hell?"

The combatants fell away from each other, spinning to face the source of the shots. Their eyes widened as they saw Colleen bearing down on them, the rifle still clutched in her hands. She stopped in front of Kel first.

"I told you I could handle this."

"Colleen . . ." he began in a voice that hovered between being stern and being cautious. He eyed the rifle uneasily. "This has nothing to do with you."

"It has *everything* to do with me," she snapped. "Do you think I don't know why you're fighting? I don't need you to defend my honor, Kelly Michael Bryan." The use of his full name was a measure of her anger and Kel looked even more uneasy.

"Colleen . . ."

"Don't you 'Colleen' me! Stay out of it!" She slammed the rifle into his midriff, butt first. Kel's hands came up to wrench it from her, even as the breath woofed out of him and he saw stars.

She was already spinning toward Gun. He watched her warily out of one good eye. The other one was rapidly swelling shut. There was a cut on one cheekbone, the beginnings of a nasty bruise on his jaw and his lower lip was split.

Staring up into his battered face, Colleen felt torn by conflicting emotions. She was furious with him.

She wanted to hate him. But the current emotion welling up inside her was definitely not hate. Angry with herself as much as with him, she drew back her fist and slammed it into his stomach. He took a quick step back, a pained grunt escaping him. She knew as well as he did that he could have avoided the blow. But instead, he'd let her hit him and that made her even madder.

"I don't know what you're fighting about. It's not your baby. There were dozens after you. *Dozens.*" Her voice rose to a shout on the last word. Seeing Gun's lack of reaction, she gave a frustrated sob and spun away from him.

Blinded by tears, she stumbled into Lije Blackhawk, who put out his hands to steady her. For reward, he got an elbow in his ribs and then Colleen was past him, snatching up the reins of his horse and swinging herself into the saddle before anyone could stop her. Not that it was likely anyone would have dared to try. Jabbing her heels into the animal's sides, Colleen rode out of the yard at a dead run.

With an oath, Kel handed the rifle to one of the men and started for his horse, which had been standing saddled and ready when he'd gotten into the quarrel with Colleen. Gun was there before him. Kel grabbed his shoulder, intending to pull him away from the animal, but Gun spun to face him, his good eye blazing with determination.

"It's my baby," he said fiercely.

After a split second's hesitation, Kel dropped his hand. Gun swung into the saddle and turned the gray in the direction Colleen had taken. A quick nudge of his heels and he was thundering out of the yard after her.

Their departure left a thick silence behind. Kel looked at the cowboys, who all looked at other things. All of them except Lije, who nodded before turning and walking toward the bunkhouse. Kel let him go, knowing Lije didn't need to hear the warning he was about to give.

"The first man who says anything about this to anyone will have me to answer to." His soft voice carried the threat more powerfully than a shout could have done. There were murmurs of agreement from the men, along with comments that no one wanted to cause any trouble for Miss Colleen.

Satisfied, Kel turned toward the house and found himself face-to-face with Megan. He stopped and eyed her warily, aware that he looked as bad as Gun. She looked at him, her expression hovering between exasperation and concern.

"Didn't anyone ever tell you that fighting's no way to solve a problem?"

"Can't say they did. My father said to make sure the other guy didn't come out looking better than you did. I think I managed that." He grinned and then winced when the gesture pulled at his split lip.

"Serves you right," she muttered, but the fingers that touched his bruised jaw were gentle. "Come up to the house and I'll patch you up."

Kel allowed her to lead him toward the house, but he cast a look in the direction Colleen and Gun had

gone, hoping it hadn't been a mistake to let Gun go
after her.

Gun knew the horse he rode was faster than Colleen's, but once he had her in sight he didn't try to
catch her. A little time to cool off would do her some
good. And it would give him time to figure out how to
persuade her to marry him.

It was half an hour before Colleen swung her horse
into the shade of a thick stand of cottonwoods that
lined a stream. Gun saw her dismount, ground hitch-
ing her horse to allow it to crop the sweet green grass
that grew near the water.

Gun walked his horse between the trees. Colleen was
sitting on the grass, her fingers tugging idly at it, her
eyes on the stream. Even if she hadn't known he was
following her, she had to have heard his arrival. But
she didn't acknowledge him in any way, even when he
sank down next to her.

Gun let the silence stretch a little and then said,
"When were you going to tell me about the baby?" He
was surprised at how calm he sounded, considering the
turmoil he felt.

"Why should I have?" she muttered, still not looking at him. "I told you already, it's not yours."

Gun's hand moved so fast there was no avoiding it.
His fingers caught her chin and turned her to face him,
giving her no choice but to meet his eyes. Colleen
stared at him, defiance and pain mixed in her expression. It was the pain that made his anger disappear as

quickly as it had flared. His fingers gentled on her skin.

"You're a lousy liar."

Her eyes flashed and she jerked her chin from his hold, but she didn't repeat the lie.

They sat without speaking for a while. To anyone watching from a distance, they would have looked as if they were in perfect harmony, enjoying the beauty of the spring day. But tension crackled between them like something alive.

It was Gun who broke the silence again. "We're getting married."

The announcement was made in such a matter-of-fact tone that it took a moment for its meaning to sink in. When it did, Colleen started to her feet, only to find Gun's hand on her arm in a hold that was as gentle as it was implacable.

"Let me go! I'd rather marry a skunk. At least they show their stripes right up front."

"I never lied to you. You may have been a virgin but you damn well knew I wasn't."

"I didn't expect you to be, but I didn't expect you to sleep with Vanessa the minute we were apart, either! Not that I give a damn what you do," she added hastily. She renewed her efforts to pry his fingers loose from her arm, but she might as well have been tugging on steel bands.

"What are you talking about?" When she didn't answer but only continued pulling at his hand, Gun caught her other arm and dragged her up onto her knees, kneeling himself to face her. "What are you talking about?" he repeated, ignoring her glare.

"You know what I'm talking about! You and...and Vanessa." Just saying their names together caused a sharp pain in her chest.

"You think I slept with her *after* I slept with you?" he demanded.

"You admitted as much!" She tried to twist from his hold, only to gasp indignantly when he gave her a quick little shake to get her attention.

"I didn't admit any such thing. I haven't touched another woman since we first made love."

"You said..." She frowned, trying to remember just what he'd said. Or rather what Vanessa had said. It was true that there'd been no specific date given. But she'd assumed...

"What happened between Vanessa and me was years ago. Good God, do you think I could have made love to you three times that night if I'd been having sex with Vanessa, too? I'm not Superman."

"Vanessa had been gone," she mentioned, but the fire had left her voice and she was no longer pulling against his hold.

"I'm only going to say this once more," he said, speaking slowly and distinctly. "I have not slept with another woman since the first time I slept with you. I haven't had the time or, dammit all, the desire." He gave her another little shake, emphasizing his next words. "*You're* the woman I want. You're the one I'm going to marry."

Colleen had been softening, but she stiffened again at the mention of marriage. "I haven't said I'll marry you."

"You will." The quiet statement made her temper flare even as a small part of her suggested that maybe her heart wasn't really in the argument.

"Just when did you sleep with Vanessa?" she demanded.

Gun's face tightened. "It was a long time ago," he said shortly. "It doesn't have anything to do with us. Tell me you'll marry me."

"Why should I?" She abandoned the topic of Vanessa, not really wanting to know the details. She would have given her soul to hear him say he loved her.

Gun considered the question, trying to decide the best way to persuade her. He could have told her that he loved her, but he doubted she'd believe him. Not after the scene with Vanessa. It was too soon. He'd wanted to find a way to get Vanessa out of his life before coming to Colleen and trying to make her understand what had happened. But the baby changed all that. Old-fashioned or not, he had every intention of his child being born with his name.

"Why shouldn't we get married?" Stalling for a little more time, he rephrased her question, making it sound as if they were considering the idea together. "We've been friends for a long time. We know we're compatible, in and out of bed."

As if to emphasize the "in" portion of that statement, Gun's fingers moved softly on her arms and Colleen felt a shiver slide down her spine. Yes, they were definitely compatible. She swallowed and grabbed for her rapidly disappearing willpower.

"Being friends and being good in bed together does not necessarily make for a marriage."

"It's not a bad start." He gave her a whimsical smile that melted bones she hadn't known she possessed. But this was her life they were talking about, the rest of her life, if she was lucky. And she wasn't going to agree to marry him unless she felt they had a chance of making it work.

"There's more to marriage than friendship and sex." She frowned. Odd, how that sounded like quite a bit when she said it out loud. Gun's raised brows suggested that he felt the same but he didn't say as much.

"You said you wanted to have something that was yours. If you marry me, the ranch will be half yours."

"Don't you mean half of your seventy percent?" She was immediately sorry for the nasty remark. Gun's jaw tightened at the reminder that the ranch was not entirely his. But his tone remained level.

"Half of seventy percent," he agreed. "Until I find a way to buy Vanessa's percentage and get her out."

Colleen liked the sound of that, particularly the tone of his voice, which suggested that his strongest feeling for the other woman might be dislike.

"It's exactly what you said you wanted, something worthwhile, a place to put down roots. It's better than enrolling in another school."

He almost succeeded in coaxing a smile from her but her teeth were too busy tugging at her lower lip to allow it to escape.

"I don't know," she whispered.

"I do. Marry me, Colleen."

He sounded so sure. She lifted her eyes to his face, searching for something that would tell her what her answer should be. And she found it in the intense blue of his eyes. The hunger there belied the calm tone of his voice.

Was it lying to herself to believe that there was something more than just physical hunger there? She wanted desperately to believe that there was. He wanted her. Maybe he even needed her. And wanting and needing could be coaxed into love.

Couldn't it?

"All right." She nodded slowly. "I'll marry you."

Gun felt something tight and hard inside him dissolve in a rush of relief. He would have pulled her close, but she pulled away from him and stood. He rose to face her. There was a stubborn thrust to her chin. Both determination and uncertainty flickered in her eyes.

"But we'll have separate bedrooms."

His eyebrows rose and he scaled back his relief a little. Obviously they had a ways to go before they got back to where they'd been. She didn't trust him, but trust could be earned.

"Separate bedrooms," he conceded. He'd have practically agreed to separate states as long as she married him.

Colleen told herself she wasn't disappointed by his easy acceptance of her terms. She'd wanted him to agree. Hadn't she?

"I guess we should head back," she said briskly, dismissing her doubts about the bargain they'd just made.

It would work out, she told herself as she swung into her saddle. Colleen glanced at Gun as he mounted Kel's horse. She was still hurt and confused. The knowledge that he'd slept with his stepmother had shaken her. The fact that it had been years before had taken the sting of personal betrayal away, but it hadn't lessened her discomfort of it.

It was one thing to know that Gun had slept with other women. It was something else entirely to actually be confronted by one of those women. And his father's wife no less... There had been no love lost between him and his father, but to sleep with Ben's wife—with any man's wife.

She shoved the thought away. She could deal with that later. Right now, what she had to concentrate on was the fact that she'd just agreed to marry the man she loved. It could have been a wonderful moment, if only he'd loved her, too.

Chapter 14

This wasn't the way she'd imagined it, Colleen thought as she stood before the justice of the peace and repeated her vows. There was no white gown, no crowd of friends watching and weeping with happiness at the joyous occasion, no flowers covering the altar, perfuming the air.

Instead, she wore a simple ivory dress with a modest sweetheart neckline and long sleeves. The bodice nipped in at the waist before flaring out in a full skirt that ended just above her knees. It was pretty and feminine and looked very bridal, Megan had told her firmly. In place of the crowd of well-wishers she'd always assumed would be a part of her wedding day, there was Kel and Megan and Michael.

Though Megan's eyes looked suspiciously bright, Kel looked grim enough to have been witnessing a funeral rather than a wedding. Gun had proven to be remarkably accurate in his assessment of what Kel's reaction would be to finding out that the two of them were lovers. What Gun couldn't have predicted was that his anger was directed almost as much toward Colleen as it was toward Gun.

Colleen stared down at the small bouquet of roses and baby's breath that Megan had thrust into her hands as they were leaving the house. They blurred together in a pink-and-white blotch and she blinked to clear her eyes. She cried too easily lately. Megan had said that it was the pregnancy that made her so weepy, but Colleen suspected it was a bruised heart as much as fluctuating hormones.

Nothing was the way it should have been. Everyone should have been smiling and happy. And Gun should have been in love with her. New tears flooded her eyes and she blinked them away, irritated by their persistence.

"Miss Bryan?" The sound of her name brought her head up and she stared at the justice of the peace blankly.

"Yes?" She'd forgotten his name. Was it Brown or Browning?

He cleared his throat and cast an uneasy glance at Gun. Colleen followed his eyes and saw Gun looking at her. There were thin white lines bracketing his mouth and his eyes were bleak. It struck her suddenly that the room had been silent for some time before Mr. Brown-Browning spoke her name. Silent, as if waiting for something. Like for her to say something.

"I do," she said hastily, feeling the color flood her cheeks.

The justice sighed with relief and hastily completed the ceremony. Colleen barely heard him, all her attention remained locked on the man at her side. When he'd heard her say, "I do," the lines had eased from his mouth and there'd been a slow warming of the chill in his eyes. He must have thought she was going to refuse to marry him at the last minute. That was why his expression had been so bleak.

Colleen felt her mood lift. If it was that important to him that they get married, it boded well for their future.

"You may kiss the bride."

Colleen felt her heart thump as Gun's hand came up to cup the nape of her neck. She'd swept her hair up in a Gibson girl twist and the touch of his fingers against her skin made her feel very exposed and vulnerable. Perhaps Gun saw something of that in her eyes because his mouth touched hers with a tenderness that made Colleen feel cherished.

One hand clutched at her bouquet but the other came up, her fingers flattening against his, feeling the solidity of muscle beneath the fabric of his coat and shirt. She forgot where they were, forgot that they weren't alone, forgot everything but the sweet seduction of Gun's mouth on hers, the steady strength of him against her.

As the kiss continued, Kel growled low in his throat and took a half step forward. Megan caught his arm, her fingers digging into the rigid muscle under his sleeve.

"They're married," she reminded him quietly.

"That doesn't mean he can kiss her like that," Kel snapped, keeping his voice low in deference to their son, who stood between them, looking bored.

Megan's brows rose, her silver-blue eyes suddenly amused. Her look made Kel realize how ridiculous his statement had been. Grudgingly, he conceded that maybe Gun did have the right to kiss his bride. But he still hadn't come to terms with the idea of Colleen as a grown woman. In his mind, she was still his little sister and probably would be even when she was nine months pregnant.

The kiss ended before Kel felt compelled to start a brawl with the bridegroom. Mr. Brown-Browning murmured his congratulations and the newlyweds turned to face their guests.

Megan hugged Colleen, unabashedly crying. Colleen's laugh was shaky and her eyes were suspiciously bright as she returned the hug. Gun would have hung back, not wanting to tread on already thin ground, but Megan wouldn't allow it. She was determined that Colleen's wedding day would be as happy as the awkward circumstances allowed.

"Congratulations." Gun returned her hug, grateful for what she was trying to do. Over her shoulder, he saw Kel approach Colleen. Her eyes were uncertain, a little pleading, as she looked at her brother. If Kel hurt her, he was going to take him out in the yard and do his best to finish what they'd started a week ago, Gun promised himself.

"They'll be all right," Megan said softly, turning to see what he was looking at. "Kel loves her a great deal." She looked at Gun, her eyes knowing. "Probably almost as much as you do."

Gun gave her a startled look. "Is it that obvious?"

She patted his arm reassuringly. "Only to someone who isn't as emotionally tangled up in all this as you and Colleen are. You should tell her how you feel."

Gun shook his head, his eyes on the couple across the room. "There are things we need to work out first. She wouldn't believe me now."

"You might be surprised at how many things work themselves out when two people admit that they love each other."

But he shook his head again. "Not this time. Besides, who said Colleen was in love with me?" His eyes slanted to hers and Megan had no trouble reading the hope in them. She shook her head.

"She hasn't said anything to me." Not that she'd had to say anything, Megan thought with some exasperation. Any fool could look at Colleen's face and know she was in love with him. She had been since she was at least eighteen and maybe before that, for all Megan knew.

Across the room, Kel had his arms around his sister, her face pressed to his shoulder. Gun felt something loosen inside him. He knew how much her relationship with her brother meant to Colleen and it had bothered him to think that he might have been the cause of a rift between them.

"I told you so," Megan said cheerfully. She linked her arm through his and tugged him across the room. "You might consider the possibility that I'm right about other things. I'm going to steal the bride long enough for us to freshen up," she announced, releasing Gun's arm and reaching for Colleen's hand.

"But I—" Colleen was dragged from the room before she had a chance to finish her protest.

The two men were left alone, except for Michael, who was kneeling on the floor making *vroom vroom* noises as he played with the little car Megan had given him from her purse. The justice of the peace had disappeared immediately after the ceremony to give the bridal party some privacy.

"I expect this is where we're supposed to shake hands and make nice," Kel said after a moment.

"I think that's what she had in mind."

They stared at each other. It was the first time they'd been alone together since the fight. Between them lay a lifetime of friendship and Kel's feelings of betrayal.

"She's my sister, dammit!"

"I know. I didn't plan on this happening."

"That's obvious," Kel snapped, referring to Colleen's pregnancy. He thrust his fingers through his hair, which was much darker than Colleen's, with only hints of red breaking through. "You should have radioed me to come and get her."

"She asked me not to. She said she wanted time to think."

"And it didn't occur to you what might happen?"

Gun hesitated, knowing he should lie. But there'd already been too many lies. "It occurred to me," he said evenly.

He saw rage flare in Kel's eyes, the same deep green as Colleen's. Kel's hands clenched into fists, and for a moment Gun thought he might throw a punch at him. But Kel regained his control.

"You should have taken care of her," he said, his voice low and fierce. "You should have protected her. You didn't even use birth control, for God's sake!"

Gun said nothing. What could he say? Kel wasn't telling him anything he hadn't already told himself. Kel couldn't think he was any more irresponsible than he knew himself to have been.

"You took advantage of her."

"No." That was one accusation he didn't deserve. Gun's head came up, his eyes meeting Kel's. "I didn't take advantage of her. What happened between us was something she wanted as much as I did."

Kel's breath hissed between his clenched teeth. Green eyes clashed with blue, and Gun knew that if it hadn't been for his son playing nearby Kel would have hit him. He even sympathized with Kel's feelings. It had been damned hard for him to see Colleen as a grown woman. It had to be much harder for her older brother to see it.

"She's not a child, Kel." It struck him as ironic that he should be giving Kel the same words Colleen had given him. "She's all grown up and she's my wife. And it would make things a hell of a lot easier on her if we weren't at each other's throats."

Kel glared at him a moment longer and then the tension slowly drained from him. "Yeah." The agreement was reluctantly given. "I guess there's not much good in fighting it at this point. Besides—" his mouth twisted ruefully "—Megan would probably have my hide."

"I'll take good care of her," Gun promised. He held out his hand. Kel hesitated a moment before taking it.

"You'd damn well better."

The damage to their friendship was far from mended, but the process of patching it together had begun.

The five of them went out to lunch in a local café. It wasn't long before the news of Colleen and Gun's marriage had spread and they barely got a chance to eat they were so busy accepting congratulations.

Not that she could have eaten much, anyway, Colleen thought later. Her stomach had been a little unstable for the past couple of days. She suspected the cause was more nerves than pregnancy. Considering the circumstances, there was no reason to think they were going to settle down anytime soon.

She glanced at Gun, who was driving them home. Her husband. For all the years that she'd fantasized about marrying him, now that it had happened she couldn't make it seem real. The small interior of his car put him only inches away. She'd only have to move her hand a little bit to brush her fingers against his thigh.

She linked her fingers together in her lap to resist the temptation to do just that. No touching, she reminded herself. It had been her idea that they have separate bedrooms, her insistence that this was going to be a marriage in name only. No matter that that seemed like a pretty ridiculous idea when his baby was already growing inside her. Or that separate bedrooms seemed more a hollow gesture than anything else. That was the bargain they'd struck and she wasn't going to tell him she'd had a change of heart.

Gun pulled the car to a halt in front of the house. He shut the engine off, but neither of them made any move to get out of the car. Colleen stared at the rambling house. The paint was peeling off the walls and there was a definite sag to the porch roof. There was no yard to speak of, only packed dirt and a few scraggly weeds.

"My father didn't put much money into the place these past few years," Gun commented.

Seeing it through Colleen's eyes, he suddenly realized how shabby the house was. He barely noticed what the house looked like most of the time. Since coming home, his attention had been focused on the things essential to running a ranch, and paint and porch roofs could wait until he had more time and money. But now he wished that he had made an effort to fix the place up.

"I'll see about getting some paint next time I'm in town," he said abruptly.

"Don't worry about it." Colleen didn't look appalled by the condition of her new home. She unbuckled her seat belt and reached for the door handle. "It can wait until the ranch is back on its feet."

Gun stared as she got out of the car. A slow smile curved his mouth as he opened his own door. He'd forgotten that she was a rancher's daughter and a rancher's sister. She knew what the priorities were. She was almost to the house when he caught up with her.

"Watch the second step. It's loose." Gun took her arm to steady her over the step and Colleen felt a shiver of awareness at even that light touch. He left his hand where it was as they crossed the porch. Colleen had an impression of scuffed floorboards and a glider that dangled unhappily from one rusty chain. The light wasn't good enough to see more but she had plenty of time to explore, she reminded herself. The rest of her life.

The door wasn't locked and the hinges squealed when Gun pushed it open. Colleen started to step inside and then hesitated. This was their wedding day. And this was the threshold of their home. She shot him a quick uncertain glance, unwilling to ask if he planned to follow tradition and carry her over the threshold.

She didn't have to ask. Gun bent to slide one arm beneath her knees, the other around her shoulders and scooped her off her feet with easy strength. Colleen linked her arms around his neck, one hand still clutching her wedding bouquet, since there'd been no one to throw it to.

He carried her inside, catching the door with one booted foot and shutting it behind them. The entryway was dim, but there was enough light for Colleen to meet his eyes. She was aware of the hard muscles of his chest pressed against the side of her breast, of the strength of the arms that held her as if she weighed nothing.

A liquid heat stirred low in her belly, a tingling awareness that spread outward until her fingers burned with it and her toes curled inside her soft ivory pumps with their neat gold bows.

His head lowered.

Her lips parted.

"Well, well, if it isn't the newlyweds." Vanessa's mocking voice shattered the moment like a hammer against glass.

Colleen was instantly rigid in his arms. Cursing under his breath, Gun set her on her feet.

"I thought you were going to Denver for a few days," he said, looking at Vanessa.

"I changed my mind." She lifted the glass of wine she held in a half toast. "I thought it was the least I could do to welcome Colleen to her new home."

"Thank you." Colleen glanced at the other woman and then looked away. She'd almost managed to forget that this was Vanessa's home, too. How was she supposed to share her house with a woman who'd once slept with Gun?

"Actually, I owe you an apology." The mockery was gone and Vanessa's low voice seemed completely sincere. Reluctantly Colleen looked at her.

"An apology?"

"For my behavior last time we met. I was completely out of line and I'm sorry I upset you." There was nothing but sincerity in her expression. She looked genuinely distressed.

"That's all right." Colleen forced a smile. It wasn't all right, but if she said as much, she'd look and feel like an ungracious little cat. Not only that, but Vanessa might think she felt threatened. And the fact that she did only made Colleen more determined not to show it.

"Thank you," Vanessa said with every appearance of genuine gratitude. "I know it's awkward, the three of us sharing a house like this, but I hope we can work things out and maybe, someday, we can even be friends." There was a little-girl wistfulness in the question that touched Colleen despite her determination that it shouldn't. Still, she wasn't going to promise anything.

"Maybe." She forced another smile before glancing up at Gun who'd been silent throughout their exchange. He was looking at Vanessa, the muscles in his jaw rigid. Though there was nothing in the least loverlike in his expression, Colleen felt a stab of jealousy so strong it almost paralyzed her. "I'm tired," she said in a voice like ice. "I'm going up to bed."

"It's barely seven o'clock." Gun dragged his eyes from Vanessa to look at his wife, his brows drawing together. "Are you feeling all right?"

"I'm fine. I'm just tired." That and she couldn't bear to see him and Vanessa together for another second.

"Are you sure?" He lifted his hand to her face, but his fingertips had barely grazed her cheek before she was pulling away. His hand dropped to his side.

Aware of Vanessa's interested gaze, Colleen forced another smile. "I'm sure. Good night, Gun. Vanessa." She nodded to the other woman before turning toward the stairs. Her things had been moved to Gun's house earlier in the day so she was spared the embarrassment of having to ask where her room was.

Vanessa's speculative look followed her until she was out of sight and then swung back to Gun. The softness she'd displayed earlier was gone and her eyes glittered with curiosity and a touch of malice. "It doesn't sound as if your bride expects you to join her tonight. Odd, considering you just got married."

Gun looked at her impassively. "My marriage is none of your business, Vanessa."

"How can you say that? We're family, Gun. The only family either of us has left."

It was impossible to tell if she was completely mocking or if there was a grain of sincerity in her tone. It was always impossible to tell with Vanessa. That was one of the things he'd once found fascinating about her. Now he simply found it annoying.

"You were never a part of my family," he said bluntly. "You made sure of that years ago."

"I don't recall you protesting." She ran the tip of one finger around the rim of her glass, her eyes going over him with a look of blatant speculation.

"I don't care about the past, but I'm warning you—"

"Warning me?" Her eyes widened. "Oooh, I like a man who's not afraid to be tough."

"—don't upset Colleen," he continued, ignoring her interruption.

"Because she's pregnant?" She saw his eyes widen a little with surprise, confirming her guess. She laughed softly. "I didn't need a crystal ball to guess that one. The little scene I interrupted a few weeks ago, now this hasty marriage. It wasn't hard to figure out you and your little cowgirl had been a teensy bit careless and got caught. I suppose her brother insisted on marriage. That's one of many things I hate about this godforsaken country, the uptight morals of most of its inhabitants. Marriage is hardly the only solution to an unwanted pregnancy anymore. There are clinics—"

She broke off with a startled gasp as Gun closed the distance between them with a speed surprising in a man of his size. His fingers closed around her wrist. He didn't hurt her, but the strength in his hand made it clear that he could snap her wrist like a dry stick if he chose.

"I don't care what you know or what you think," he said, his voice soft yet deadly. "I don't care that you own part of this ranch. If you upset my wife in any way, I don't care how small, I will twist your miserable head right off your skinny neck and bury you so deep that not even God will be able to find you. Do I make myself clear?"

Vanessa stared up at him, all the masks momentarily stripped away to reveal the stark fear in her eyes. When she didn't answer, he tightened his fingers infinitesimally.

"Do I make myself clear?"

"Yes."

The word was hardly more than a breath but it was enough to satisfy him. He released her arm and stepped back. "I'm working on getting the money to buy out your portion of the ranch. In the meantime, mind your own business and stay away from my wife and we should manage to rub along together."

He didn't bother to wait for a reply, but climbed the stairs two at a time, leaving Vanessa to stare after him.

She wasn't afraid of him. He wouldn't really hurt her, after all. It was just idle threats. But her hand was trembling as she lifted the wineglass and gulped down its contents.

Chapter 15

Colleen was amazed to find her life quickly falling into a routine of sorts. No matter what the emotional turmoil she felt, life still went on. There were still meals to cook, dishes to wash, cattle to be fed. Not that she was doing any of the latter.

She frowned, remembering Gun's reaction when she'd suggested helping with the ranch work. You'd think he'd talked to Kel, she thought irritably, because he'd trotted out the same argument. She was pregnant. As if she needed to be told. The fact that pregnant women were riding horses and working cattle all over the state didn't seem to impress him. He had said he wouldn't be able to concentrate on anything else if he knew she was endangering herself and the baby. No amount of arguing could change his mind and Colleen had finally given in, at least temporarily.

It wasn't as if there wasn't more than enough work to occupy her in the house. Luckily she actually enjoyed housework, even if it wasn't fashionable to admit it. And Gun's home—her home now—had been neglected for so many years that even a small expenditure of time and effort resulted in a spectacular improvement.

A week of hard work had the house looking as if someone not only lived in it but might actually care a little about it. That same week of essentially mindless labor had given Colleen plenty of time to think about anything and everything, both of which seemed to boil down to Gun and their marriage.

One week and one day into her marriage, she ran the vacuum over the threadbare carpet in the upper hall, considering the possibility that she was occasionally too clever for her own good. Separate bedrooms had seemed like a good idea when she'd agreed to marry Gun. She'd had some vague idea that keeping a physical distance between them would foster the emotional closeness she hoped to find in her marriage.

Instead, it had become simply the most obvious symbol of the distance between them, a distance she didn't know how to bridge. Aside from the argument over her riding out to work the ranch with him, she and Gun had barely exchanged two words since the wedding. It wasn't a hostile silence, but that didn't make it any less impenetrable. In all the years she'd known him, she'd never had any trouble finding things to say to him. But now, whenever they sat across the table from each other, her mind was a complete blank.

Not that their meals were silent. Vanessa made sure that didn't happen. She always seemed to have something to say and she didn't need much encouragement to say it. Her conversation generally centered around herself—her travels, her friends, her wardrobe. Colleen suspected that at least some of the apparently aimless chatter was directed at herself, that Vanessa was ever so subtly pointing out her own sophistication and, by default, Colleen's lack thereof.

For the most part, Colleen ignored the transparent attempts to undermine her confidence, but there were other things about Vanessa that were not so easily ignored. First and foremost was the other woman's past history with Gun. It didn't matter that he showed about as much interest in Vanessa as he did in the furniture, Colleen still couldn't shake the image of the two of them together.

The other problem with Vanessa was that she never lifted so much as a finger around the house. She shouldn't have been surprised by that, Colleen reminded herself, remembering the condition the house had been in. Obviously Vanessa had no interest in housework. She spent most of her days in her room, watching television, chatting on the phone and putting endless coats of polish on her nails.

It wasn't that Colleen cared whether or not Vanessa scrubbed a toilet or mopped a floor. But it was bad enough that the woman was living with them without having to deal with her interference in the day-to-day running of the household. And she had no intention of becoming Vanessa's housekeeper, either.

This morning, for the second time, Vanessa had asked her, very nicely, if she'd mind vacuuming Vanessa's room while she was doing the upstairs. The first time, Colleen hadn't really minded. It had seemed a not unreasonable request. After all, she had the vacuum out, what was one more room? By the same token, when Vanessa's clothing had appeared in the laundry room, it had seemed a little childish to sort them out and leave them in a heap on the floor.

But after a week of hard work, during which Vanessa had not offered to so much as dust a shelf, Colleen decided it was time to put a stop to the little game they were playing. She wasn't the naive little country girl Vanessa thought she was and she had no intention of letting herself be used. She'd briefly debated the possibility of direct confrontation and then decided that guerrilla tactics offered more room for creativity.

She reached the end of the hall and flicked the vacuum off, unplugging it and coiling the cord around the handle before carrying it to the linen closet. She patted the bag fondly before closing the door on it, feeling well pleased with her morning's work.

It was nearly dark before Vanessa sought her out. Colleen was sitting in the newly cleaned living room reading a magazine when she heard the sharp click of Vanessa's heels on the stairs. Vanessa had to be the only woman in the state of Wyoming who wore high heels at home.

"Have you seen my diamond earrings?" Vanessa asked by way of greeting as she walked into the living room.

Colleen took a moment to mark her place in the article she hadn't been reading. She lifted her head and gave Vanessa a puzzled look.

"Diamond earrings?" she repeated slowly, as if not sure what the words meant.

"The diamond earrings that were on my dresser this morning when you came in to vacuum."

Accusation hovered beneath the surface of the words and Colleen felt her temper stir. As if she'd ever wear anything that had belonged to Vanessa.

"I don't remember seeing them," she said, maintaining her dull country-bumpkin facade. Vanessa's jaw knotted with irritation and she turned away, only to spin back around when Colleen continued, speaking slowly as if she had to think about the words.

"I did bump into the dresser, now that I think about it." She frowned a little. "And I'm not sure but I thought I saw something shiny on the carpet afterward. I didn't pay much attention, really. I just thought it was a bit of foil or some such thing."

Vanessa's fair skin paled to the color of parchment and her eyes bulged with horror. "You vacuumed up my diamond earrings?"

"I don't rightly know." Colleen smiled apologetically, hoping the light wasn't good enough for Vanessa to see the laughter in her eyes. "Like I said, I didn't see what it was."

"I can't believe you'd vacuum up a pair of diamond earrings!" Vanessa pressed her hand to her chest, as if the thought had brought on palpitations, which Colleen suspected it had. "My God, do you know what they're worth?"

"Couldn't even guess," Colleen admitted cheerfully. "It's not a tragedy, though. If it was them I saw, they're still in the vacuum cleaner bag. I've heard that diamonds are pretty hard. Being sucked up in a vacuum probably won't have done them a lick of harm."

"You expect me to go through the vacuum cleaner like a ... bag lady?" The idea made Vanessa's brows climb so high they nearly disappeared into her hairline.

"I guess it all depends on how much you want your earrings back." Colleen shrugged and opened the magazine as if the topic had lost her interest.

She stared at an ad for a photographic safari to Africa, listening to the sound of Vanessa's harsh breathing. Out of the corner of her eye, Colleen could see the woman's hands clenching into fists at her sides and knew Vanessa wanted nothing more than to do her some physical injury.

After a moment, Vanessa spun around and left the room. Colleen heard her heels tapping rapidly up the stairs and a few minutes later the sound of the vacuum thumping against the stairs and, from the sound of Vanessa's muttered curses, occasionally thumping against her shins. By the time the back door slammed behind the other woman, Colleen's grin was so wide it was almost painful.

She resisted the urge to go into the kitchen and peer out the door to see what Vanessa was doing. If Vanessa saw her, she'd realize that vacuuming up the earrings hadn't been an accident. And Colleen wanted a little more revenge before open warfare broke out between them, as it almost certainly would. It was enough to know that Vanessa was sitting out there, her lily-white hands buried in mounds of dirt and lint as she searched for her precious diamonds.

Colleen was still savoring her victory when she heard the back door open again and the solid thud of Gun's boots on the floor as he entered the house. Despite the problems between them, her pulse sped up. Her fingers trembled on the magazine as he entered the living room.

"What's Vanessa doing on the back porch? It looks like she's playing in a pile of dirt."

Colleen shrugged. "She said something about losing a pair of earrings." Her expression was innocent as she looked up at him.

He was filthy from head to foot, even his blond hair had streaks of dirt in it. There was a three corner tear near the knee of his jeans and his shirt pocket dangled loose on one side. He looked absolutely gorgeous.

"You look like you've had a rough day," she commented, wishing she could go to him and put her arms around him, filth and all.

"It wasn't too bad." He thrust his fingers through his hair, grimacing at the dust the movement generated. "I feel like that character in the Peanuts strip, the one with the dirt cloud following him around."

"Pigpen?" She smiled. "You look a little like him."

"Thanks."

She looked so beautiful, sitting there with her hair tumbling around her face and smiling at him, that it was all Gun could do to resist the urge to snatch her up off the sofa and kiss her until she forgot the whole idea of separate bedrooms. They were married, dammit. She was so beautiful, just looking at her made him ache, and he was supposed to keep his hands to himself.

That was the deal, Larsen.

And a damned lousy one at that.

"I'd better get cleaned up," he said, not sure he'd be able to stick to the deal if he kept looking at her.

"Gun."

He turned, surprised that she'd delayed his departure. She hadn't shown any particular desire for his company this past week, in bed or out. They rarely saw each other except at meals, and even then she was usually quiet, letting Vanessa do most of the talking.

"Are you very tired?" She ran her fingers restlessly up and down the edge of the magazine she held.

"I'm not about to keel over from exhaustion. Is there something you need?"

"Not need. Not really, anyway." She shot him a quick look from under lashes. "If you aren't too tired, I was wondering if we could have dinner at the café. It's Friday night and I thought it might be nice to go out. Unless you're too tired."

"I may be a few years older than you are but I'm not standing on the edge of the grave yet. I think I could probably manage to get these old bones as far as town."

"If you're sure." She looked almost sorry that she'd suggested it, but Gun wasn't letting her back out now.

"I'm sure. Give me twenty minutes to clean up."

He turned and left before she could tell him she'd changed her mind, if that was really what he read in her eyes. Taking the stairs two at a time, he felt his muscles protest. The truth was, he *was* tired. When he'd walked in the house, all he'd wanted was a hot shower, a meal and a bed. But this was the first time she'd actually sought his company and he'd have risen from his deathbed rather than refuse her.

Nineteen minutes later, he was walking back down the stairs, buttoning the cuffs on a clean shirt. His hair had been toweled partially dry and combed into place. It would finish drying on the way to town.

As he reached the bottom of the stairs, Vanessa stalked out of the kitchen. She was wearing a pair of pearl-gray tailored slacks and an aqua-colored silk blouse, both smudged with dirt. Her hands were utterly filthy, as were the cuffs of the blouse. One hand was clenched as if she held something in it—the earrings Colleen had mentioned, he assumed.

"Vanessa." His polite nod received what could only be termed a snarl in return. She brushed past him and stalked up the stairs, her heels slamming into each and every step. Gun turned his head and saw Colleen standing in the living room doorway, her head tilted to watch Vanessa's departure. There was a gleam in her eyes he couldn't quite interpret. Above them, Vanessa's door slammed with ringing force.

"Problem?" He'd meant what he told Vanessa. He wouldn't allow her to play her malicious games with Colleen. If she was causing trouble, he wanted to know about it.

"I don't think so," Colleen said calmly. "I certainly hope she found her earrings."

Something in her voice suggested that he was missing a vital piece of the story, but he chose not to pursue it. He didn't want to talk about Vanessa tonight. This was the first time since their marriage that Colleen had actually sought out his company. The last thing he wanted to do was talk about another woman.

The evening had been a success, Colleen decided several hours later. It hadn't gone quite the way she'd envisioned, but it had been a success nevertheless. She'd first thought of going out for dinner as another way to annoy Vanessa. If Colleen wasn't available to cook, the other woman would either have to cook for herself or go hungry.

But then it had occurred to her that spending a few hours alone with Gun might help break down a few of the walls between them. That those walls were mostly of her own building didn't make it any easier to reach past them.

If she'd wanted time alone with Gun, it had been a mistake to go the café. On a Friday night, the place was crowded, mostly with local ranchers and their families, most of whom knew Colleen or Gun or both. Everyone wanted to say hello to the newlyweds, to offer congratulations and good wishes.

But maybe the evening had turned out better for the interruptions, she thought now, as they were driving home. It had taken some of the pressure off. They hadn't dealt with the problems between them, but she thought they'd regained a little ease with each other.

Other than their wedding lunch, it was the first time they'd gone out together as husband and wife. After hearing herself addressed as Mrs. Larsen a few times, she was almost starting to feel married.

She gasped as his car bumped over a rut in the road, rattling the passengers.

"Sorry." Gun glanced at her, his mouth twisting ruefully. "This thing isn't much good on bad roads."

"No, but it's beautiful." She patted the leather interior. She wasn't much of a car fancier herself, but she knew Gun had put a lot of hours into the sports car. When he'd bought it, it had been almost a wreck and he'd restored it himself.

"Yeah, but not practical." He pulled into the shed that served as a garage and turned off the engine. He slid out and Colleen did the same. They met at the back of the car. "I've got a friend in California who thinks he's found someone to buy it."

"Oh, Gun, no!" Colleen looked at him in dismay. "You put so much work into it. You love this car."

"Yes and no." She caught the quick gleam of his teeth in the moonlight. "I did put a lot of work into it and I'm proud of it." He glanced at the car as he pulled the shed doors shut behind it. "If I hadn't inherited the ranch, I'd have kept it, but it's worth a lot of money and I want the money more than I want the car."

"It seems a shame, though. All that work." Colleen pulled her light jacket closed. It was spring, but the nights were still cool.

"If it will help get Vanessa off the ranch, it will be well worth it."

"I can't argue with that." It was worth almost anything to accomplish that.

Gun put his hand on her arm, stopping her just short of the front steps. Colleen turned to look up at him. The moonlight bleached his fair hair to almost white and shadowed his eyes. Just looking at him, she felt her heart swell with love.

"Has she been giving you trouble?"

Her thoughts had been so far away that it took her a moment to drag them back to the conversation. She shook her head.

"Not really. Nothing I can't handle, anyway." As she thought of Vanessa's dirt-smeared manicure, her mouth curved in a pleased smile.

"Why do I get the feeling that Vanessa may be the one with the problem?" Gun's eyes narrowed when he saw her contented expression.

"I have no idea." She widened her eyes innocently and batted her lashes a time or two, delighted when his smile widened into a grin. For the first time in weeks, she felt completely at ease with him.

Snow Bride

He was still holding her arm and his fingers moved against the sleeve of her jacket, his thumb shifting in an absentminded caress that, even through the layers of fabric, sent shivers down Colleen's spine. He seemed to feel the same thing or perhaps he felt the sudden awareness in her. His smile faded, his eyes becoming more intent.

"I had a nice time tonight," Colleen said, rushing into speech to cover the nervous flutter of her pulse. *When had he gotten so close?*

"Yeah."

"It felt odd, hearing people call me Mrs. Larsen." His head dipped toward hers and she forgot how to breathe. "I guess I'm not used to being somebody's wife," she babbled.

"Maybe you need a few reminders." His breath brushed across her mouth.

"Gun." She didn't know whether it was protest or welcome. Her hands were clinging to the rough denim of his jacket, though she had no memory of reaching for him. "Gun."

"What?" But his mouth closed over hers, smothering her reply.

Colleen's knees weakened as his tongue slid along her lower lip, asking and receiving entrance to the honeyed sweetness beyond. It had been so long, she thought, crowding closer to him. So long since he'd held her like this, kissed her this way.

His tongue swept into her mouth, claiming her, filling an emptiness that was more emotional than physical. His hands were strong against her back, crushing her body to his with gentle strength, drawing her into the notch of his spread legs. She could feel the firm pressure of his arousal, feel an answering emptiness in her.

"Colleen." Her name was a whisper against her cheek. He kissed her again, stealing her breath, nearly stealing her wits. "I've missed you so much."

"Me, too." She felt his hand slide into her hair, dislodging the combs that held it back from her face, tumbling them to the ground. She didn't care. She could find them tomorrow or let the winds bury them. She couldn't drag her eyes from Gun's face, all shadows and angles in the moonlight.

"Come to bed with me," he whispered against her jaw. "Let's forget separate bedrooms. It was a stupid idea to start with. Come to bed."

If he hadn't said it was a stupid idea, Colleen would undoubtedly have gone with him without so much as a whisper of protest. But it had been her stupid idea that they have separate bedrooms and she felt her back go up a little at his blunt assessment.

Gun felt her stiffen and knew he'd lost her, at least for the moment. A wave of overpowering frustration roared through him. The past week of having her as his wife yet not his wife, of seeing her every day yet not being able to touch her, of knowing every night that she was sleeping just a few feet away and not being able to go to her, had left his mood a little shaky.

And now, to have her pressed against him, to feel the hunger in her and know she wanted him and yet have her pull away...

He lifted his head and glared down at her in the moonlight. "Dammit, Colleen. We're married. Or were you trying to forget that?"

Stung, she pulled back as far as his hold would allow and returned glare for glare.

"*I'm* not the one who has a history of forgetting wedding vows," she snapped.

The minute the words were out, she wished them unsaid. But it was too late. Gun released her as if she'd suddenly caught fire. Even in the thin moonlight, she could see that he'd paled, could see the sudden rigidity of his jaw. He took a step back and she was suddenly terrified that, if he walked away now, she'd lose him forever.

"Gun." She reached out, drawing her hand back without touching him. "I'm sorry. That wasn't fair."

"Why not? It's the truth." His voice was flat and hard.

"I don't know what the truth is, but I know I had no right to say that to you."

"If it's what you think—"

"It's not. I swear it's not." She pressed her hands to her cheeks, fighting the urge to cry. "I'm sorry," she said again, her voice trembling.

"It's okay." She saw his mouth curve in a quick, meaningless smile.

It wasn't okay. She didn't know what had happened between him and Vanessa, but she knew it haunted him, and she shouldn't have thrown it in his face like that. But the words couldn't be taken back.

After a moment, Colleen sighed. "I guess I'll go up to bed."

Gun said something about checking on one of the horses and they exchanged stilted good-nights before Colleen went into the house, leaving him alone with the moonlight and his ghosts. She climbed the stairs slowly. There was nothing waiting for her but a lonely bed in a lonely bedroom.

And she had no one to blame but herself for that. If she hadn't let her temper get the best of her, Gun would have been with her and she could have been spending the night in his bed, in his arms.

Soon, she promised herself as she shut the door to her room and leaned back against it. Very soon she'd find a way to reach through the barriers created by her stubbornness and his pride and make this marriage as real as it already was in her heart.

Chapter 16

The progress Colleen had thought she and Gun had made in the early part of their evening out had been nullified by its tense ending. The next morning he was gone before she came downstairs and she didn't see him again until dinner, at which time they seemed to have returned to the polite distance that had thus far been characteristic of their marriage.

The frustration of it made her want to scream and the knowledge that she had no one to blame for the situation but herself did nothing to improve her mood. She knew the first move was going to have to come from her. What she didn't know was what it should be or how she was going to come up with the courage to make it.

But if there were still kinks to be worked out in her marriage, there was at least one area of her life where things were going exactly as she'd hoped.

"That was a brand-new bottle of Chanel No. 5," Vanessa said. Her jaw was so tight, Colleen was surprised she could open her mouth wide enough to get the words out at all.

"Oh, no!" Colleen looked properly horrified. "I'm sorry, Vanessa. But it was right on the edge of the sink and I just didn't see it. I was mopping and my elbow bumped it. You know how it is when you're working, you just about need eyes in the back of your head. It might not have broken if it hadn't hit the edge of the tub like that." She'd never realized how difficult it was to break a perfume bottle until now. It had taken half a dozen tries before the stupid thing shattered.

"Do you know how much a bottle of Chanel No. 5 costs?" Vanessa had the dazed look of an accident survivor.

"No, but I feel just terrible about breaking it." Since Vanessa had her own money from investments made before she married, Colleen wasn't worried about her ability to buy another bottle of perfume. It wasn't easy to look regretful but she managed it. After a moment, she let her expression brighten as if an idea had just occurred to her. "I have a bottle of Desert Flower perfume you could have. It's practically new. Megan gave it to me for Christmas this last year."

"Desert Flower?" Vanessa's voice came out on a croak.

"It's a real pretty scent," Colleen said, looking like a hopeful puppy.

"Desert Flower?" This time it was a shriek. "You want me to wear Desert Flower instead of Chanel No.

5. If that stuff costs ten dollars a gallon, they're over-charging. Chanel is two hundred dollars an ounce!"

"Two hundred dollars!" Colleen's eyes went wide with shocked disbelief. "Goodness, for that much money you'd think they'd put it in a nice plastic bottle so you wouldn't have to worry about breaking it."

Vanessa moaned in pain.

"Oh my God!" Vanessa's scream echoed through the house. Colleen grinned as she glanced up from the pie crust she was rolling out. Over her head, she heard the sound of a closet door slamming and then the rapid tattoo of Vanessa's high heels as she ran from her room. A few seconds later, she burst into the kitchen.

"You ought to be careful coming down the stairs so fast in those heels," Colleen commented without looking up from her task. "You could take a nasty fall."

"What do you think you're doing?" Vanessa's voice hovered on the edge of hysteria.

"I'm making a pie for dinner. Coconut cream. It's Kel's favorite and I thought Gun might—" She broke off, startled by the feel of Vanessa's hand on her arm, spinning her away from the counter.

"Don't think I don't know what you're doing," Vanessa said, her dark eyes glittering with rage. "I'm not fooled by this stupid act you're putting on. You're doing this deliberately."

"Take your hand off my arm while you still have it to take." Colleen's voice was like steel. She saw surprise flicker in the other woman's eyes, whether because of her tone or because she didn't deny her accusations she didn't know.

"Fine." Vanessa's hand fell away from her arm. The other hand rose, holding a crumpled bundle of white fabric streaked with pink. "This was a Donna Karan original."

"Should I gasp in awe or merely fall to my knees in worship?"

"You deliberately ruined it."

"I washed it. It was in the laundry so I washed it."

"It has to be hand washed. It says it right on the label." Vanessa's fingers shook as she jerked at the label in question. "Can't you read?"

"I can read." Colleen reached behind her and picked up a towel, using it to dust the flour from her hands. "Did you honestly expect me to do your hand washing for you, Vanessa?"

"I don't see why not. You could add it to yours."

Colleen stared at her for a moment in disbelief and then leaned back against the counter with a laugh. "You really are incredible."

The genuine amusement in Colleen's laugh brought angry color to mottle Vanessa's elegant cheekbones. "You deliberately ruined my blouse."

"Yes, I did," Colleen admitted without hesitation.

Vanessa's mouth dropped open in shock. She stared at Colleen, her mind working rapidly as she considered the torments of the past two weeks. "My perfume," she whispered.

"Those bottles are damned hard to break."

"And the spiders in the bathroom. I thought they'd come in through the window."

"I spent a good part of an afternoon catching them."

"My earrings! You deliberately vacuumed up my diamond earrings!"

"You shouldn't leave valuable things laying around," Colleen said without remorse.

"How dare you!" Vanessa sputtered a moment but couldn't come up with anything more substantive so she repeated herself. "How dare you!"

"It's not hard. I want you out."

"This is my house."

"Only thirty percent of it."

"I have rights."

"I'm not preventing you from living here. But I'm not under an obligation to make it pleasant for you, either."

"I'll sue you!"

"For what?" Colleen grinned. "Do you really want to go to court and explain that you expected me to do all the cooking, all the cleaning and wash your clothes by hand? I don't think you'll get much of a sympathy vote."

"You little bitch!"

"Coming from you, I can almost consider that a compliment."

"I won't stand for this."

"Then you can sit for it. But I want you out of my house and I want you out of Gun's life." The minute she said it, she knew it was a mistake. She shouldn't have mentioned Gun. Vanessa pounced on the revealing words.

"Worried that he still finds me attractive?" she asked, regaining some of her customary poise. "You should be. Gun and I were *very* good together and I'm sure he remembers that as well as I do." She smoothed one delicate hand over her hip. "I'm not moving out, no matter what you do, and in a few months you're going to be fat as a cow and about as attractive. I'll be here, available, and I'll make damned sure Gun knows it. Meanwhile, you'll be sleeping in your born-again virgin bed all alone."

Vanessa's smile widened in a malicious grin when she saw her barbs had gone home. "I don't think coconut-cream pies and Suzy Homemaker skills make up for an empty bed. Not for a man as virile as Gun. And we both know just how virile he is, don't we?"

With the final purred comment, Vanessa turned and left, taking her ruined blouse with her.

Feeling as if she'd just been hit with a sledgehammer, Colleen groped for a chair and sat down. Maybe letting her antagonism come out in the open hadn't been such a good idea. She was just so tired of dealing with the woman.

No. Be honest, Colleen. You can't stand the thought of her living in the same house with Gun. That's the real reason you've been making her life a misery.

Colleen put her elbow on the table and leaned her face into her hand, forcing herself to face the truth of Vanessa's words. She was scared to death that Gun found Vanessa attractive. Never mind that he showed no interest in her, that he actually seemed to dislike the woman. Never mind that, despite what had happened between him and Vanessa, Colleen didn't believe he was the kind of man who'd break his wedding vows, even when she did get fat as a cow. But those were logical arguments and logic had nothing to do with the fear she felt.

She and Gun were so far apart right now. What if they never found their way back together?

The solution is in your hands, a small voice whispered inside her. *Or at least the beginnings of it.*

Sleeping together wouldn't magically solve their problems, but as long as they had separate bedrooms their marriage was just a facade. Marriage was built on a foundation of trust and she'd made it clear she didn't trust Gun. If she wanted out of the stalemate they were in, she had to be the one to make the first move.

Colleen heard Vanessa go out the front door and then the sound of her car driving away. She chewed on her lower lip. Vanessa seemed determined to stay on the ranch, at least until she got her thirty percent out of it. It was bad enough to think of having to live in the same house with the woman, without having to lie awake nights wondering if she was trying to sneak into Gun's bed. One sure way to cure that worry was to make sure Gun's bed was occupied. By his wife.

Setting her chin, Colleen got up, pulled off her apron and left the kitchen.

* * *

Gun rubbed his hand over his face, grimacing at the grittiness of his skin. Satan had picked today to be in a particularly nasty mood. Ordinarily Gun recognized the signs and knew to be on guard when he was on or around the big horse, but today he'd been distracted, and Satan, with all the craftiness of his namesake, had taken the opportunity to throw him butt first into a pile of brush.

The damned horse had then headed for home, leaving his owner to walk a mile and a half in boots designed for riding. If he'd had a gun, he'd have shot the ornery piece of horseflesh, he thought as he limped into the ranch yard and saw Satan in the corral, calmly eating hay. Bill Granger was seated on a bench next to the bunkhouse, making repairs to a bridle. He looked up as Gun limped past.

"Figured he'd throwed you. I was just debatin' whether or not to come lookin' for you."

"Thanks," Gun said sourly.

"Horse like that—a rider's got to stay awake," he commented to no one in particular. "Don't pay to be gettin' distracted."

Gun didn't bother to reply but only continued to make his way, somewhat painfully, to the house. These days he was permanently distracted. Two weeks of marriage and he was letting his horse throw him. Another month like this and he'd get himself killed.

He entered by the kitchen door, pausing long enough to draw in the rich scents of roasting meat and coconut pie. He couldn't say that Colleen didn't set a good table. He'd eaten better in the past couple of weeks than he ever had in his life. But there was more to life—and marriage—than food.

Gun took off his hat and hung it on the hook next to the door before limping across the kitchen and heading upstairs. They had to get this worked out. He'd come to that conclusion during the interminable walk home. He didn't mind giving Colleen time—all the time she wanted—as long as there was some point to it. But it had been two weeks and they'd barely exchanged two words. He didn't know what Colleen expected, whether she was waiting for some bolt out of the blue to tell her that the time had come to share his bed or if she wanted him to court her. If it was the latter, he was willing. If it was the former, they had a problem.

Gun stalked through his bedroom without slowing and went into the bathroom. Turning on the shower, he adjusted the water to something just short of scalding and stripped off his clothes, letting them fall where they would. By the time he stepped into the shower, the bathroom was filled with steam.

He stood under the stinging spray, letting the heat ease the aches from his bones while he tried to formulate just what he'd say to Colleen, just how he'd persuade her to give up this notion that sleeping apart was going to accomplish something for their marriage.

He considered Megan's advice to tell Colleen that he loved her, but he wasn't sure she was right. He didn't want Colleen to think he was saying he loved her just to persuade her to share a bed with him.

Frowning, Gun turned off the water and stepped out of the shower. Vanessa's car had been gone, he remembered as he reached for a towel. Maybe it was an omen and he and Colleen could talk tonight. He toweled the moisture from his body and, rubbing a towel over his wet hair, walked out of the bathroom.

And found himself face-to-face with Colleen.

Time seemed to freeze in its tracks.

Colleen's fingers tightened around the stack of panties she'd just carried in from her room. She'd intended to put them in the drawer she'd cleared for that purpose. She'd heard Gun taking a shower, of course, and she'd known that he'd be out soon. She'd been gearing herself up to tell him that she was moving her things into his room, that the separate-bedrooms idea had not been a particularly good one. She'd had her speech all planned.

But she hadn't expected Gun to walk out of the bathroom completely, and magnificently, naked.

Her eyes went over him compulsively, taking in the heavy strength of his shoulders, the damp mat of hair on his chest that narrowed to a fine line of dark gold curls that led her eye across his tight stomach to his thighs. She swallowed hard, unable to drag her gaze from him.

Gun felt himself stir and begin to harden beneath the fascinated green of her eyes. Her tongue came out and licked nervously at her lower lip and it seemed as if he could almost feel that light touch on his flesh.

"I ... I was just ... I thought ..." She seemed to be having a hard time putting together a coherent sentence. Not that it mattered because he didn't think he could put together a coherent response.

"I hope you're moving that stuff in here," he managed hoarsely.

"Stuff?" She dragged her eyes upward and looked at him blankly. When he nodded to the crumpled armful of nylon and lace, she blinked at it as if she couldn't remember how she came to be holding it. "I ... was moving my things. In here. To your room."

"Good." Two long strides brought him to her. "It's about time we had a marriage to go along with the license."

"Yes."

His hands slid into her hair, tilting her face for his kiss. Lacy undergarments rained onto the carpet as Colleen threw her arms around his neck. This was what was needed to fill the empty space in her heart. This man, holding her, loving her. With a soft groan, Gun bent and lifted her in his arms to carry her to the bed.

"As wedding nights go, I think this one must have broken a few records," Gun said against Colleen's hair. Her body was draped across his, one leg nestled intimately between his thighs, her hand lax on his chest.

"You were right—separate bedrooms was a stupid idea," she admitted.

It was after midnight and they'd loved, slept a little, made love again and slept again. When they woke the second time, they had made their way downstairs to dine on overcooked pot roast and coconut pie. Now, back in Gun's wide bed, they lay cuddled together.

Colleen felt as if she couldn't get close enough to him, as if she needed to make up for all the weeks they'd barely touched.

"I tried to tell you it was a stupid idea," Gun said sleepily. "Ouch! That hurt." He tilted his head to frown at her.

"Sorry. My hand slipped." Colleen rubbed her fingers over the chest hair she'd just tugged. "I've noticed that people who say 'I told you so' seem more accident-prone than those who don't."

"I'll keep that in mind," Gun said, eyeing her warily.

They lay without speaking for a little while, just enjoying being together. Gun ran his hand up the length of her back and was not surprised to feel desire stir again. It seemed as if he could never get enough of her.

"Tell me about Vanessa."

His hand stilled on her back. "That's ancient history."

"I know. And I know it shouldn't matter because it happened long before we were involved."

"Then why ask?" Gun rolled away from her and sat up on the edge of the bed.

"Because I can't let it go until I know what happened." Colleen sat up and stared at his taut back. "I know you're not the kind of man who'd sleep with a married woman. Especially not—"

"Especially not his own father's wife? Is that what you were going to say?" He stood and reached for his jeans, pulling them on with impatient jerks. The rasp of the zipper sounded loud in the quiet room.

"Well, I did sleep with her," he said harshly. He turned to face her, his face all hard angles in the lamplight. "No excuses. No lies. I slept with my father's wife."

Colleen reached for the sheet, pulling it up in front of her, suddenly uncomfortable with her nudity. "I have to know," she said quietly.

"Why?"

"So I can let it go. Please, Gun. I already know the worst. Just tell me what happened."

He stared at her, his eyes tortured. She thought he was going to refuse and she wasn't sure what she'd do then. But then his shoulders abruptly slumped.

"All right." He ran his fingers through his hair, looking suddenly very tired. "It's really not all that interesting. My mother died when I was fourteen and my father remarried less than a year later." He'd already told her that much when they were in the cabin, but Colleen didn't try to rush him.

"I'd just turned fifteen when he brought Vanessa home. She was twenty-three or so. She'd been a model and I thought she was the most beautiful thing I'd ever seen."

Colleen felt jealousy twist sharp and tight in her chest. Maybe she didn't want to hear this, after all. But there was no stopping it now.

"I liked Vanessa. She was fun and there hadn't been a whole hell of a lot of fun in my life lately. I was almost as tall as I am now and years of working the ranch had put a lot of muscle on my frame. It made it easier for her to treat me as a contemporary. We spent a lot of time riding and talking. I'd never had anyone listen to me the way she did or talk to me like I was an adult."

He shook his head, his mouth twisting in bitter memory. "I fell in love with her, of course."

"Of course," Colleen repeated weakly. She was definitely sorry she'd asked.

"My father treated her better than he did most people he knew, but he was a cold sonofabitch. He seemed to hate me. Maybe it was because I was young and he wasn't or maybe he really did hate me, but he started trying to push me into fights."

"Fights? You mean physical fights?" Colleen couldn't imagine a father and son trading blows.

"Physical fights. I think he felt like he had to prove himself against me, against someone young and strong. Maybe he was trying to prove something to Vanessa, that she might have married a man thirty years older than she was but that he was still stronger than a man a third his age, even if it was his own son."

"But that's awful!" She forgot her concern about Vanessa in her indignation against his father. "That was a terrible thing to do to you."

"I survived." He shrugged, dismissing what had happened. "Vanessa always patched up my bruises and scrapes and she seemed genuinely upset about what he was doing. It's hard to picture Vanessa as an angel of mercy, but that's how she seemed to me. I'd never had any real affection for him, but I really started to hate him. I hated the way he treated me and I hated the fact that he treated Vanessa like she was a pet on a leash. I thought she deserved so much more."

He stopped, apparently lost in memory. Colleen felt her heart twist with fear. Had she made a terrible mistake, forcing him to relive memories from a time when he'd cared for Vanessa?

He seemed to shake himself, and his voice became more clipped. "They'd been married almost a year when I turned sixteen. My father had gone to Montana to look at a bull he was thinking of buying. He hadn't remembered my birthday but that didn't surprise me. But Vanessa remembered, and when I got home that night she had cake and ice cream and a present for me—a rifle I'd had my eye on. She opened some wine and we drank the whole bottle."

He stopped again and Colleen saw his throat work as if he was swallowing something bitter.

"What happened?"

"We ended up in her bed," he said in a flat voice. "I thought I'd died and gone to heaven. Not just the sex, which was probably pretty lousy. Even lousy sex seems great to a sixteen-year-old kid. But I thought it meant that she loved me. I laid awake until dawn, planning how we'd run away together. I'd ride rodeo until I could get us a stake to buy a place of our own. Oh, yeah, I had it all worked out."

His hands clenched and unclenched at his sides and Colleen noticed that his shoulders and chest were damp with sweat. She wished she'd never asked him to tell her what had happened, wished she'd simply let the past stay in the past. But there was no stopping the flood of memory now.

"Of course, the inevitable happened. It was like something out of a bad movie. I fell asleep. My father got home early and caught us in bed together. If he'd had a gun, I think he'd have shot us both. I sprang up and dragged my pants on, standing between him and Vanessa, telling him we loved each other. God, I must have looked like a fool." He rubbed his hand over his face as if trying to rub away the memory of his own youth.

"What did Vanessa do?"

"Vanessa? Vanessa did what Vanessa does best— she looked out for herself. While I was busy proclaiming my undying love, Vanessa began screaming like a banshee, sobbing that I'd raped her."

"Oh, God." Colleen put her hand to her chest, feeling her heart twist with pain for the boy he'd been.

"My father believed her—at least, he chose to pretend he did. He dragged me out of the house and proceeded to beat me half to death. He told me I had half an hour to get myself out of his house and if I ever set foot on his property again he'd shoot me on sight."

"But he must have realized he was wrong or he wouldn't have left you the ranch. He must have been sorry."

"Sorry? Ben Larsen didn't know the meaning of the word." Gun's laugh was bitter. "No, he didn't leave me the ranch by way of apology. He left it to me because I was blood. He knew I hadn't raped Vanessa, but it proved a convenient way to get rid of me. And leaving me the major portion of the ranch was as good a way as any to punish her for every crime she'd ever committed and I imagine she committed more than a few during their marriage."

There was a short silence and then he released a short, angry breath. "Are you happy? Do you feel better, knowing the whole ugly story?"

"Yes." Colleen nodded slowly. "I do feel better. Now that I know what happened—how young you were and the way she used you—I don't have to worry that you might still be in love with her."

The eyes she lifted to him were clear green and so full of love that Gun felt his heart stop.

"Love Vanessa? You didn't really think that, did you?"

She looked down, shrugged a little. "I wondered a time or two. She is beautiful."

"If you like the reptilian type." He braced one knee on the bed and reached out to slide his fingers into her hair, tilting her face up to his. "How could you think I loved her when you had to know that I loved you so damned much it was killing me." It was as if something tightly held had suddenly loosened inside her, spilling light and warmth over every corner of her being.

"When?"

"For a lot longer than I was willing to admit." He ran his finger over her cheek, savoring the feel of her skin. "When I fished you out of that snowbank and carried you into the cabin and then had to help you undress, it was a kick in the gut to see that you weren't the little girl I remembered. I couldn't stop thinking about you. No matter how many times I told myself to keep my hands off of you, all I could think about was touching you."

"I tried hard to encourage that feeling," she admitted smugly.

"You succeeded." He leaned down to brush a kiss across her mouth, tasting the love in her response. It had always been there, he realized with some surprise. He'd just been too blind to see it. Or maybe he hadn't seen it because he thought he didn't deserve it.

But reliving old memories had done more than reassure Colleen. It had made him realize that it was time to stop blaming himself for past mistakes that had not been his alone. It was time to let the past go and get on with the future.

His hand came to rest on her still-flat stomach. This was his future. This woman and this child.

"Don't you have something you'd like to say to me?" he whispered against her mouth.

"You're overdressed." She tugged impatiently at his jeans.

He lifted his head to frown down at her. "I had something a little less earthy in mind."

Colleen nibbled her lower lip, pretending to consider. "Oh, that's right." She linked her hands around his neck, giving him a smile brimming with happiness. "I love you, Gun. I've loved you since I was eight years old, which is a great deal longer than you've loved me."

"I guess I'll just have to work hard to make it up to you," he said against her mouth.

And he proceeded to start doing just that.

Epilogue

It was only a matter of weeks before Vanessa departed in a cloud of Chanel No. 5 and anger. With Colleen and Gun standing solidly together, she couldn't cause mischief, her chief form of amusement. The coup de grace came when Colleen cheerfully pointed out that, with the baby's birth, Vanessa would be a grandmother and would she prefer to be called Grandma or Gran? The suggestion was enough to drive the color from Vanessa's elegant face.

Almost immediately, she decided to accept Gun's offer for her thirty percent of the ranch. Without a twinge of regret, he handed over the money he'd gotten for the sports car and they watched Vanessa drive out of their lives.

It took Kel a few months to come around, but the fact that Colleen was glowing with joy in her marriage, as well as the nearly thirty years of friendship he and Gun had shared, brought him around. Besides, once he and Megan found out that they were going to have another child, it just wasn't possible to hold on to old anger.

Seven months later, Gun and Colleen welcomed their daughter into the world. Katherine Mary Larsen was born in the midst of a snowstorm, which seemed only appropriate since she'd been conceived in the aftermath of a blizzard. Her father's hands were the first to touch her, to lay her against her mother's breast. Through eyes blurred with exhaustion and joyful tears, Colleen looked from her tiny, perfect daughter to Gun. Her heart was so full of happiness, it almost hurt to breathe.

Since she was eight years old, Colleen had known that she and Gun were meant to be together. It had taken her sixteen years to bring him around to her way of thinking but it had been well worth the wait.

*   *   *   *   *

Dark secrets, dangerous desire...

Lovers DARK AND DANGEROUS

Three spine-tingling tales from the dark side of love.

This October, enter the world of shadowy romance as Silhouette presents the third in their annual tradition of thrilling love stories and chilling story lines. Written by three of Silhouette's top names:

LINDSAY McKENNA
LEE KARR
RACHEL LEE

Haunting a store near you this October.

Only from ❤ *Silhouette*®

...where passion lives.

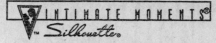

**And now Silhouette offers you
something completely different....**

**In September, look for
SOMEWHERE IN TIME (IM #593)
by Merline Lovelace**

Commander Lucius Antonius was intrigued
by his newest prisoner. Although spirited
Aurora Durant didn't behave like any woman
he knew, he found her captivating. But why did
she wear such strange clothing, speak Rome's
language so haltingly and claim to fly in a silver
chariot? Lucius needed to uncover *all* Aurora's
secrets—including what "an air force pilot lost
in time" meant—before he succumbed to her
tempting lures and lost his head, as well as
his heart....

INTIMATE MOMENTS®
Silhouette®

SILHOUETTE®
Desire®

They're sexy, they're determined, they're trouble with a capital *T*!

Meet six of the steamiest, most stubborn heroes you'd ever want to know, and learn *everything* about them....

August's *Man of the Month*, Quinn Donovan, in
FUSION by Cait London

Mr. Bad Timing, Dan Kingman, in
DREAMS AND SCHEMES by Merline Lovelace

Mr. Marriage-phobic, Connor Devlin, in
WHAT ARE FRIENDS FOR? by Naomi Horton

Mr. Sensible, Lucas McCall, in **HOT PROPERTY**
by Rita Rainville

Mr. Know-it-all, Thomas Kane, in **NIGHTFIRE**
by Barbara McCauley

Mr. Macho, Jake Powers, in **LOVE POWER**
by Susan Carroll

Look for them on the covers so you can see just how handsome and irresistible they are!

Coming in August only from Silhouette Desire!   CENTER